All Things…..

"Camus' *Outsider* meets the Marquis de Sade. Darkly compelling..." Andy Martin, author of *Waiting for Bardot*.

All Things Considered

Clifford Thurlow

Bastard Books

Bastard Books
(A division of Usualready Enterprises Ltd.)

Published in Great Britain by:

Bastard Books
(A division of Usualready
Enterprises Ltd.)
85 Clifton Hill,
London, NW8 OJN.

First Edition

A CIP catalogue record for this book is
available from the British Library

PUBLISHERS NOTE

This is a work of fiction. Names, characters
places, and incidents either are the product
of the author's imagination or are used
fictitiously, and any resemblance to actual
persons, living or dead, events, or locales is
entirely coincidental.

ISBN 1-84346-001-7

For

Antonio Lobo Antunes

One

"Helena."

"Tomas?"

"Yes, it's me." I was whispering, I realised.

"Tomas?"

"Yes."

"It's so late."

"It's not. Everything's all right," I said.

"What?"

"It's all right, now."

"What do you mean?"

"I can't explain. A car's coming."

"A car?"

"I should make the next flight."

She paused. "I'll meet you."

"You will?"

"Yes, Tomas." Again the pause. "Tomas, are you all right?"

"Yes. Yes, I am. "

"I'll be waiting for you."

"Thank you."

I hung up. A car horn sounded outside. From the balcony I could hear the shriek of sirens, the toll of the cathedral bell, a distant crackle like static. I ran down the stairs with my case. I wasn't taking much.

"The airport," I said.

The driver threw my luggage in the boot. He stared at me for a moment. I thought he was going to acknowledge who I was, but merely shrugged and climbed into his seat.

He pulled away, headlamps dimmed against the murky night. The streets were empty except for the fire trucks and police cars. There was a thread of light on the horizon, a faint glow that could have been the dawn but it was still too early. I could smell burning and ran my fingers instinctively under my nose. My hands smelled of smoke. They have always smelled of smoke. There was the stub of a cigar in my pocket, which I lit.

People were standing at their windows staring into the night. Clouds hung in the sky, a dark curtain stretching over the hills, the stench unpleasant, but no worse than that to which we have grown accustomed. It will pass. There was a job that had to be done and I have done it. I feel no regrets. To be honest, beyond a mild sense of relief, I don't feel very much at all.

It has been a long night, a night when decisions were made, breaking from their shells like extinct birds from the glass cases at the museum.

Why this night?

There's no answer. Everything's random. I had returned home as usual and stood on the balcony feeling vaguely annoyed about nothing in particular. I could hear the widows talking next door. They were taking the air, a rash occupation, but in habit they had found the will to carry on.

I glanced at my watch without registering the time. I was dying for a drink.

Two

The balconies, crescents of wrought-iron where climbing plants once grew, face west and we look out with private memories at a fading sun peering from the sky like the eye of a fish from deep water. The far hills, naked without their bonnets of snow, are grey and tortured, like the teeth of the senile matelots who sit wreathed in pipe smoke on the harbour wall keeping watch for ships that no longer come. The evening remains warm, even now, in winter.

Odd words pass through the iron lattice that divides us, a giggle, the price of food, a mild rebuke. They are the widows of a colonel and captain who served in the same regiment and maintain a stubborn observation to their relative rank. They never mention the weather but dwell still in those ephemeral, starlit moments below chandeliers in a throng of débutantes with slender waists and puckered lips, the flush of young breasts heaving with innocent optimism. Madame Sorulos, the captain's widow, is frail and carries a hump, but she must have been pretty once. She shrouds the growth beneath a voluminous cape that gives her a theatrical appearance and I want to reach for the mound when she passes and touch it for luck. The colonel's widow is tall, shrivelled, like the trunk of a dead tree, her long dresses, once black, turning green, as if with a coating of moss, a reflection of the clouds that nest among the hills. She has a nose and chin that grow more pointed as her skin recedes, a moustache modestly embroidering her top lip as if in honour of the brutal growth the colonel wore. Her name is Madame Raimonde. It is on the door, above Madame Sorulos; two old women who have remained behind because they have

3

nowhere to go and we cross on the long climb up and down the stairs with feigned cheer and mutual gasps for a vanishing supply of oxygen. We soldier on. I go to the office each day. They hurry through the empty streets with an unfettered greed for the little ersatz cakes they carry home in white boxes tied with string. They take tea at four when the newspapers arrive and give a gratuity to the concierge when he brings them to the door. He bows his head as if to relish the shine on his good leather shoes and pockets the coins like a rodent collecting for hibernation.

The night tastes of baby sick and burnt fat. I cough before going inside where the air is no better, but the staleness is at least my own. I am still fit, considering everything, and at an age that is neither old nor young but at that point when we begin to sense the first stale odours of middle-age; a hesitancy in the water's flow. It is a time when the years are too many and too few for serious renegotiations with fate; the time when we see ourselves ageing in the faces of our friends, in the grey swallowing Anton's beard, in the bald spot he diligently tried to hide.

It was a small vanity Sofie forgave him, as she forgave the procession of first year girls who populated the past, weighing his roll of misdemeanours against those few brief weeks of love with Michel, Anton's brother, before he left for good, an atonement for her husband's small sins, that one big sin of her own.

"Have I committed incest?" she asked Helena wistfully, and my wife replied: "Haven't we all?"

Helena's pale blue eyes had the ambiguous look of an old china doll, her long sardonic face exacting in its symmetry, her cheek bones

4

casting purple shadows over the hollows of her cheeks. She was tall, angular, almost awkward. I never tired of looking at her.

We were at one of the Cesar's Friday soirées on a night like many nights I had imagined I wanted to forget and find myself remembering with inexplicable clarity. Their apartment, unsold, naturally, lies two floors below our own, a distance too short for me to ever find an excuse not to go.

Sylvie and Alun, the Cesar children, raced across the drawing room, round as tennis balls in striped pyjamas, Nanny limping in their wake hissing Teutonic threats. There was music from the Andes, a lament for pipes and the past. Anton was on the balcony among the eager and innocuous, the high priest of his own opinions. I was half listening to the women while I watched him over a glass of Bulgarian champagne, his latest discovery.

"The Swiss, my dears, would find it *brut*," I heard him say and there were peals of laughter.

Sofie was glowing in the light of the art-deco lamps with that irrepressible euphoria only an affair can inspire. She had dressed with the dishevelled care of the young and immodest, her hair a shade lighter, the chestnut brown of our student years submerged in streaks of gold and copper, colours of autumn.

After steering Helena to a corner, she breathlessly shared the intimacy of her transgressions, Helena's gaze straying around the room as if in search of some insignificant item momentarily misplaced.

Later, after the party, while I was flossing caviar from my teeth, she casually mentioned Sofie's confession.

"It doesn't surprise me," I said.

"Why?" she asked. I met her study in the mirror. "Were you listening?"

I paused. "It was in her eyes."

Helena finished removing her clothes and stepped between the sheets. "How old's Michel?"

"He must be ten years younger than Sofie," I replied.

"That explains it."

"What?"

"A younger man makes it all seem worthwhile."

"The voice of experience?"

Lines marked her brow. "Sofie told me."

She smiled. Her arms were arched behind her head, pushing her hair over her face.

"Do you always divulge your friends' secrets?"

"Only if they are interesting," she said.

I joined her in bed. "A reminder of your own virtue. Or a salve against future treachery?"

"Nothing is how it seems."

"What if it is?"

"No, Tomas. It would just be too tedious."

She bit my neck and throat, pinning me down. We made love, swishing through the sheets like two fish in shallow water.

We were happy, as Sofie that night had been happy. She could forgive Anton; forgive him everything: the Biedermeier furniture that filled his office, the vintage Mercedes, the art books published by the university and bought in bulk with her own money to make him appear more successful than he was. He did pay grateful homage to his wife's fortune, but what he craved was the great public feeding from the drip of his average intellect.

I can picture him now and do so: the bottle of Bulgarian bubbly, the bow tie and avoirdupois. Let me tell you what that bow tie actually meant: it said he was a teacher first, an artist never.

"Paint something that will make us feel unsettled," he told each intake of new students and they nodded their heads like bobbing boats that have found a safe harbour.

You did have style: a manly hand-shake, nothing fishy or limp; a ready smile, good teeth, a kiss for all cheeks, an ear sprouting hair for all those intense skinny girls dressed in black, nomads in their own undiscovered universe. Your gift, Anton, was your charm, that sleight of hand; eyes twinkling, dark and liquid, staring out through half-moon glasses with all the callow energy of the aspiring painters you seduced. That pot belly lurking like a park flasher beneath the capacious folds of a colourful waistcoat, camouflaged like the monkish pool of bare flesh below the fabric of your back-combed hair; those arms with hirsute wrists emerging from a cashmere jacket, extended with the expansive gesture of the celebrity you so dearly wanted to be.

Anton, did you ever buy a book by an unknown young writer? Or read one?

I'm sure he saw my faults as well as I saw his. He must have known my plan for the Palace had been more arrogant than romantic. My regard for the practical aspects had been scant at most, the social I hadn't even considered. It was a flight of fancy on a drawing board, a picture book palace drawn from atavistic dreams that led with all the

7

certainty of cause and effect to those solemn moments when I lay on my bed listening to the motions in the adjoining room and masturbated below the print of Munch's *The Cry*. I kept a box of tissues at hand. The shutters were closed. The walls shadowy. The hours as long as time spent waiting for someone who fails to appear and, with the vague satisfaction of a small job successfully executed, I would return to the makebelieve palazzo with the peculiar melancholy that comes from jerking off with no one in mind.

It was before Anton had discarded Helena for Sofie, long, long ago and yet, even then, I often awoke from a nightmare where I wandered through the coiled labyrinth of a deserted city.

Like the fleeting kiss of an artist at a vernissage, the light over the horizon has gone and I pour the warm night its first glass of wine. Two white moths circle the light bulb. My bureau is awash in litter, like the quiet foreboding streets, the echoes of my cough coming back from the vacant spaces where Helena's clothes had hung; her shoes had stood: red, blue, green and yellow, like pairs of myna birds in a display case. Her image drifts over the tarnished mirror at the end of the hall and sometimes I turn and it appears she is there but I only see myself, tall and stooped as if ready to apologise. There are bruised circles below my eyes. Plough lines dig the thin soil of my brow. My hair recedes. I have the sorry look of someone caught in the act of a petty offence.

Is this hyperbole, the exaggeration owed to the first sip of wine?

I am a tall man with sloping shoulders, grey eyes, greying hair and the dusty grey suit of one who, after an eternity of exemplary behaviour, has neglected to make a more courteous introduction.

Forgive me. I am Tomas Sala, state architect, as you are no doubt aware. I am, I imagine, the best-known architect in the land, a position attained solely by chance, as Professor Cesar finally revealed through the long green tunnel of an empty bottle, relieving himself of this awesome load like a widow at the grave of a bullying husband.

I had not been entrusted by providence with some special gift, like Gaudi or Richard Rogers, but had been sucked like a little heap of iron filings upon the magnetic whim of our First Minister. The Lion, like an exile who follows the culture notes in week old newspapers, had acquired a sudden passion for the arts. He examined the fibreglass trees, the cupolas and spires, the crenellated battlements, the vast whispering halls of my auto-eroticism. He read in my verticals, diagonals and horizontals a message encoded in stone (such are dreams) and, taking my visions as his own, I was transported from the steps of graduation and placed in an office where I could make those dreams come true.

I feel inclined to chuckle. It is at my own expense. You see, even in those days, with the millennium hanging about us like a pestilence, the trees had been drawn with the ink of subtle mockery. Even then, the woods were disappearing. Which made the giant elms that lined Victory Avenue all the more surreal and magnificent, the high branches entwined like the arms of policemen at a food riot, the wide trunks speckled brown like the marks that patterned the First Minister's hands and are growing now on my own.

How quickly the wine glass empties. I should eat. One of the dancing moths has cremated itself on the light bulb and the other contemplates the same diversion. With the darkness comes a new layer of silence, a

9

deep, humming, expectant silence like the faint pulse one imagines there will be inside a coffin.

The rooms are stocked with cases of wine and lingering demons, Helena, my parents, Cristian, his voice dimly present in the sepulchral space where the telephone seldom rings and the only sound that meddles with the calm is the radio turned on at this time every night by the mesdames widows, the far away strains of a string quartet tapping against the windows like insects curious by the light.

I always try not to listen and the fact that I always do brings back the same memory: the headboard in the next room at university beating against the wall as Anton delicately removed another hymen. Your words, were they not? I like to turn them over, you confided to anyone who would listen. You haven't had a woman until you've had her up the arse.

It reminds me of the old joke: Did you sleep with your wife before you were married?

No.

I did.

You had Helena first. There were even times when I wondered if Cristian were yours. But Helena was too old by then. It was virgins you wanted to turn over so you could burst upon their secret little gardens with all the tyranny of my Palace upon the public park, taking something away forever.

The wine's going to my head. I should eat. My freezer's full of meals for one: Fish Special, Chicken Tikka Masala, Super Vegetarian, Beef Bonanza, Soya Supreme, Noodle Surprise à la Italiana and they all taste the same regardless of claims as bold as war news that they are newly improved and contain more, though the colourful cartons grow smaller not larger. They are time-saving. Just remove the reconstituted cardboard sleeve, place the dish on the circular platform and: *ding-ding.*

Wait a moment. There. Look at that: no mess. I'm easing the quaking square of sustenance on to a china plate. There's lots of steam, that indefinable smell you find in the streets of industrial towns, the light from the microwave insipid and apt.

I eat in the dining room, Helena's favourite room, with its carpet a pattern of pale blue like her eyes, with the tall blue vases on the curved mantel; the fire was lit for dinner parties though it made the room too hot, misting the gilt mirrors staring down upon a round mahogany table, its platoon of a dozen chairs in an equidistant ring like the digits of a clock. I am never sure where to sit and, circling the table, I become aware of myself in an infinity of images where, due to minute distortions in the mercury-backed glass, I progress into buffoonery as well as oblivion.

I maintain certain standards. I brandish a knife and fork, intricately hall marked, and the food tastes ingeniously of nothing at all. I use a paper napkin that I spread out, refold and work through my fingers until it disintegrates into snow flakes as fine as the cobwebs that move over the apartment's high ceilings. I wear a grey tie on a shirt with a collar so soiled only incineration would clean it. I remember my father once saying philosophically that, while alone, one should act as if they were in the presence of a respected guest, words that come back to me whenever I sigh or fart. He also said you should trust your own instincts, as dumb a suggestion as most of those

11

adages. The tortoise is ponderous, not slow. Foxes are rarely sly simply persecuted. And dogs are their own best friend.

I was recently attacked by a pit bull terrier, a white one with a coat of sores and a pirate patch over one of its pink eyes. It managed to take a piece out of my leg before its keeper shuffled up, beat the animal with a length of piping and put a chain around its neck. "Trouble is, they've got no brains," he said cheerfully. "No brains at all." And off he went, warmed by this exchange with a stranger.

It's a curious thing but it is the workers, if that's what they're still called, who enjoy keeping killer dogs, and I suppose many find them a comfort, living the way they do. I had thought that particular breed had been banned, then I meet one and it bites me, a superficial wound, although a bruise emerged in a circle of pale teeth marks and my trousers I threw away.

The widows were in the lobby when I arrived home, Madame Raimonde directing a long tapering finger like a conductor's baton at the sign on the concierge's office: Gone To The Bank.

"Dear Mister Sala you're limping," said Madame Sorulos, her head bent to balance her hump, eyes like the scratched glass eyes of Cristian's Teddy bear.

"A dog took a nip at me in the park."

"The man's never here, Mister Sala. What are we going to do?"

Madame Raimonde's lips vanished into the tunnel of her mouth as she spoke. She scribbled something on the note, then buried her pen in a wilted leather bag with a clasp that rasped like indigestion.

"I beg your pardon?" I'd forgotten the question.

She lowered her voice. "Have you seen that gypsy woman with the baby?" she asked. "She pricks it with a safety pin. It's a trick, you

12

see. To make it cry. We have to be careful with these people." She glanced about her before going on: "The doorman we had when the Colonel was alive retired at forty: a millionaire."

Her thin body shook like a reed as she took a breath and recomposed her features.

"Come Mimi, we shall be late," she added and I opened the door. Madame Sorulos lumbered along behind her companion like a grotesque shadow. I reached out to touch her but hesitated.

"Good day, Mister Sala," she whispered, and they were gone.

My meal, still too hot to eat, has the appearance of an orange dinghy on the ocean of my plate, a flavescent paste, something recycled, like the carton. Perhaps it is the carton? The steam clinging to the mirrors has the sulphurous smell of the air outside only more acrid and it makes me cough, a cough that, in the stillness, has the sound of a prisoner hammering on a cell door.

In the dining room, away from the mournful strains of my neighbours' music, there is utter silence and, as I eat, I begin to imagine I am the only person on the planet. Everyone has gone and I have been left behind like a character in a story; the crippled boy who remained in Hamelin.

There must be many here among us who spend our entire lives waiting for a spaceship to land and for some ethereal being to step out with a beckoning hand and human lips that frame the word "Come." Come with us. Come away to a new and better world where you can start again, be young again; a world where Cristian rides a bicycle, where there's no smell of sulphur, no moss-furred clouds that hang so low you can reach out from the balcony and grab cloying handfuls,

13

sticky as an oil slick. In this world you'll find snow on the hills, the trees fill the eye as far as the horizon, the fields and orchards are fashioned into a quilt by hedgerows and it is all watched over by a farmhouse with a wood-burning fire, the little sprigs of smoke suspended on a sky that is blue not yellow.

The chairs gathered around me are straight-backed, starkly elegant, suggesting their affinity to Helena, who chose them: eleven companions as hushed as the disciples once Judas had gone about his task. We remain motionless, in a state of deep trance, spiritualists at a séance who wordlessly call out to a wandering soul that is myself. I had been able to see the table and chairs in countless reflections while I had been standing but, sitting, all I see are walls of silvered glass that reflect themselves and nowhere is there a glimpse of a man hunched over a foggy dinner plate.

I search on odd occasions through the dusty rooms for some token that reminds me of me: a footprint, a recent photograph, the stub of a cigar, a letter leaning against the clock, a note from the cleaning woman to say the cleaning has been done.

The cleaning has not been done. The maid has gone and the apparatus she left behind, pails, mops, brooms, an ironing board, stand in disarray at one end of the kitchen like an exhibit of dinosaur bones, like Helena's cello reclining in its stand in the music room with its bay of tall windows that collected the sun and made her skin diaphanous as she played Elgar's Cello Concerto in E minor.

Three

It occurs to me that there is something I should do, I must do: *I will do*.

The end of a journey starts at the beginning: my room at university, green twilight in the chestnut trees, Anton next door - I like to turn them over, he said, and I often visualised those perfect little bottoms when I made love with Helena and I wondered what it was that occupied her imagination. I began our relationship merely as an ear. Helena was in love with Anton with the first flush of love from which a woman never fully recovers.

"And now he just ignores me. He ignores me and I feel stupid."

"He's like that."

"I keep thinking he's laughing at me. We used to talk for hours about all the things I'm interested in, about books and music and morals and Max Ernst. We talked about the role of the artist in a new century. We understood each other. I told him everything about myself and he told me everything about himself. And now he ignores me."

She broke off, leaning her head to one side, the cloak of her hair sweeping over her features like a curtain at the end of a play's first act. In film terms this was the *hook*. As I looked back at Helena, I was crossing the first threshold. The story had begun. Would I be the hero of my tale?

"He told me he had been hurt," she was saying. "He made me feel sad. He said he was trying to get over someone and he didn't think he ever would..."

- He's a bastard. He says that to all the virgins. He told me himself.

Words, I confess, I did not say.

I listened, a sympathetic cast to my eyes, the swelling in my jeans so firm against the denim I could have done permanent damage to all the fine tiny tubes of my reproductive system and probably did.

"He told me I was in love with him. He was so sure of himself. He said I had the soul of an artist. He saw it in my expression when I played. He said artists can only discover themselves through struggle and pain. It was like finding something that had always been missing. He had become my friend, my best friend..."

And thus he took her little prize.

We were sitting on the far side of the park that was soon to vanish beneath the subconscious murmurings of my ambition. The geese were hollering. The sun was going down over the trees.

"I..." I began.

She put a finger to my lips. She understood something young boys do not understand and young girls do. It is the female of the species that chooses, makes marriages, builds dynasties. A blue shadow like an incoming tide swept over the grass. We were alone. Night falling. For three weeks he'd been passing her and she was eighteen with a short skirt and white pants as fragile as a cream meringue. I parted the screen of her hair. Her febrile eyes were glossy with unshed tears - of rage? of joy? of bitterness? She laid back and, when we made love, we were both thinking of Anton Cesar.

At least I was. We never know what anyone else is thinking and it is just as well.

16

I once had a friend named Rolf. We frequented jazz clubs in the Old Quarter. We sat up all night analysing rock songs, Zen koans, the malicious genius of the Tao: 'The common people often fail on the point of succeeding.' When he went abroad as a photographer we corresponded with e-mail enthusiasm. When I went on study trips to Egypt and Greece, it was Rolf who received my thoughtful postcards. We had known each other from childhood, bonding on bicycle rides and fishing jaunts. He was a friend of Helena, as we both befriended the chain of lovers and wives who hauled him through the years; women who dressed as gypsies and had souls rooted in the bourgeoisie.

One summer, back from somewhere, a beard decorating his cheeks, a new bride with hennaed hair on his arm, Rolf borrowed my car to make a journey across country and it was stolen. My insurance company, through one of those miracles of small print, failed to pay up. I neither complained nor suggested Rolf contribute towards the cost of replacing the car. Neither did he offer. The summer became winter. At Christmas I sent him a book by an unknown author. Rolf never responded and we never saw each other again.

A melancholic tale? On the contrary. It was a relief. We had not been weaving a magic carpet to carry the minds of two kindred spirits. We had thrown a meagre bridge over a yawning chasm and that is the basis of most association.

The incident even made me appreciate what I had with Anton, which was nothing. I felt a tepid indifference towards him while he, I believe, nurtured a secret if subliminal envy of me. It was sufficient for lasting friendship.

Rolf, now I come to think of it, was like Anton in many ways, but with something missing. Anton acted on instinct. He wanted to fuck virgins, then roll them over and fuck them more thoroughly, much as a healthy dog wants to mount every bitch in heat. Rolf lacked this animal integrity and desired women in numbers, much as the nouveaux riches crave paintings by known painters on their walls whether they understand them or not.

Friendship is expendable. It fulfils a function at a given time and time moves on. The companion on a hiking holiday, the business partner, party comrade, all become our inseparable soul mate. Then the tide goes out and we are left marooned on the shoreline with the dead fish and used syringes. Do you remember friends from school and college? We shook hands and swore oaths. We believed we would remain close for the rest of our lives and we look back through the decades and where are they? Wraiths across the road whose eyes we avoid; passing promises to meet for lunch; dead from a heart attack at forty-two; men turning fat and bald, or grey and thin, alone in silence with their food growing cold and welding itself like vomit to the bird pattern on a china plate.

I forage around the edges. It is truly, religiously remarkable. I am eating a baked polystyrene cup, a sort of substitute porridge, a sham baby food infused with chemicals and rays, something false and hopeless. Like friendship.

Let me pour you another drink.

Why, thank you.

A toast - to Anton Cesar.

I was grateful to him when Helena let down the white butterfly wings clasped to her brave little flower and allowed me to enter that moist and barely seen kingdom. It was fey and confused. In and out, my creamy seed with its taste of lemon and ricotta spreading like milk from a bottle over the vault of her stomach with its steep curving ridges of sculptured bone, leaving stains that sequinned her skirt like islands on the surface of an uncharted sea.

She smiled and the faint shrug that went with that smile made me think of a patient shop assistant with a customer who buys nothing. I wasn't sure whether I should thank her or apologise. I mopped away the spilled milk with a clean pressed handkerchief sent weekly in a package by Mother and thought about the Palace growing more detailed on my drawing board.

We sauntered home. The trees were shifting silhouettes against the hills. Was there a slight swagger in my walk? I would boast of my conquest, marry Helena, and regret boasting when I met those bald-headed fellows I promised to meet for lunch. She held her chin high and took long, boyish strides. I placed my arm around her shoulders and she slowed, glancing at me with that swift, sideways look that seemed to say some decision had been made.

Neither of us spoke. We left the park, ambling through pools of pallid light that led like stepping stones into the misty distance. The story of Anton's seduction, an account I had heard before, and would hear again from others, had culminated in a few fumbled seconds of clumsy lust and I wondered if we had been closer before the event than after. We picked around the periphery of our youthful limitations in search of something to say and, as all vanity leads to self-contempt, all words in the vacuum led to Anton Cesar, her first lover and ex-best friend.

"Have you seen the work he's doing?"

"A lot of it's derivative," I replied.

"He says the same about your designs."

"He misses the point, the satire."

She slowed, turning to look at me again. "In music we keep rearranging the same notes to compose new music. Its very nature is derivative."

"I just think it lacks a certain honesty. He's not trying to create something because he feels it in his soul. He just wants to be something."

"Everyone wants to be something."

"Do they?"

"No," she said.

She was quiet for moment. "The mannequins are amusing. They're so..."

"Kitsch?"

"Under stated."

"Under dressed," I said and she laughed and I had never heard her laugh before. Girls giggle but grown women seldom laugh.

We had broken away as we walked but now she slipped her arm through mine, forging a link, and she was with me and I was with her and we were no longer with him.

Until the following Saturday when his one-man show opened at a gallery in the Old Quarter and the whole world came to stand at the feet of Anton Cesar.

Laser music, shrill as a fractious infant, was clamouring for attention. Champagne Bellinis stood waiting in glasses as tall as Texan débutantes, peach gold; effervescent. Fat people picked at peanuts and vol-au-vents thin people disdained. A claret red carpet covered the stone floor. Ashtrays shaped as steamships floated on wire stems, swaying as if in a tempestuous sea, puffing out smoke. Camera bulbs flashed. The lights were pink; flattering. Everyone was there and what they saw was what they had become...

"...a transmutation into relative form," a thin man with black hair was saying. He turned to me. "Don't you agree?"

"I'm not sure."

"He has taken a natural concept that pre-empts all need for interpretation."

His companion, a black man with lots of hair, glossy as live eels, handed out cigarettes with golden filters. "While pursuing imagery as a representation of idées fixes," he said, "Anton accepts, as did Titian and Van Gogh, that reality is real."

"Portraying the virtue of matter over mind," added his companion.

"Post-maximalism, yet so light hearted."

"Just another plagiarist?" I suggested.

"Aren't we all, dear!" I was told.

I left the pair. Molecules of chatter buzzed about me like mosquitoes at sunset. I was looking for Helena while I studied the pieces. I was faintly impressed. Anton Cesar, twenty-four, still a student, had taken a mirror and on its surface was revealed the glittery wrappings of the time's passing package.

He glided across the gallery with Sofie.

"Kiss. Kiss."

"Lovely show," said the black man with eels for hair.

Anton hid his delight and appeared sombre in a dark suit, an unbuttoned shirt lazily displaying the curly dark hair on his barrel chest, a square jaw with freshly-trimmed beard denoting an oikish determination, a narrow brow awaiting the tug of evolution.

Helena appeared.

"Kiss, kiss."

"Fabulous," she said and he put an arm around her shoulders with that proprietary gesture great men have for the women they roll over and Anton that day had for the entire universe. Sofie occupied his free side and, with both arms outstretched, he looked like a sublime if well-fed Christ at ease with his Cross.

"Tomas, do have a vol-au-vent," he said and Sofie found this terribly amusing.

He took one himself, freeing Helena for a moment. Someone handed me a joint rolled in parchment. I was looking now at a woman like a black swan in a black dress cut to expose everything normally hidden. She was leaning against a wall, one foot raised behind her, talking to a short, sallow man in a burnous and Turkish fez. Her eyes met mine and made them water.

"If that's your taste, *she's* a *he*," Anton whispered and wandered off.

A voice like a fret saw started up behind me and I turned. "He has taken the strands of hedonism and erotica to knit a coat of many moods." It was a woman in tan suede, ancient and powdered below a leather sombrero, pulling me to one side, picking at my sleeve with red claws like painted chicken's feet. We stared into a glass case

22

where, on a maroon velvet cushion, lay a gold Rolex watch. The title was a very large sum in American dollars.

On the walls hung the emblems of Mercedes, Jaguar, Ferrari, in giant size, sprayed silver. He had arranged a thousand ties on a board and called the piece Hèrmes. On a plinth under perspex was a Chanel bag; on another, spiked heels by Gucci; an ingot of gold with the metal prices on the international market. Anton had dressed the mannequins Helena so admired in the creations of Cerruti, Gianfranco Ferre, Valentino, the slaughtered Gianni Versace, placing them on a cat walk in such a way the voyeur could catch a glimpse of their plaster genitalia ornamented with the snippings from his beard after "two hours of fellatio with a really juicy one."

Which one?

I glanced around the room: Sofie, the latest; Helena, the previous; Lolita, the one before?

The music grew louder. The gallery owner was Argentinean, a tiny, boyish man who trembled faintly as he took the hands of the young, lingering with their fingers as if to extract the adolescence from their tender flesh. "Thenthathional," he said, and we sucked in our cheeks and nodded with wise approbation.

"Late kitsch and so reminiscent," squealed the old gaucho in a voice from another century, leather fringes flapping, snail tracks of sweat coursing over powdered cheeks, broken blood vessels emerging like patches of coral on the raked beach of myriad facelifts.

"Ani Ivancheva," she confided, offering me an oyster shell hand and lowering curled lashes like dried larvae over her black magic eyes in the modest way of one known by name not sight.

23

While others would one day be dipping their Mont Blancs in vitriol, she was among the few critics who would praise my work and with the despicable presumption that it would place her in the good graces of the Lion.

I took her shrivelled offering. "Tomas Sala."

"You're a student?"

"Of architecture."

"A builder of illusion from the palette of stone."

I smiled. She lowered the dead lashes with a coy sensuous shrug and drew closer. "Had the Rolex been real, I would have said the next step had been taken," she began, favouring me now with a sermon that had the ring of a cherished piece of music played often in lonely rooms at ungodly times.

"The purpose of Art is to make us see the familiar through new eyes. It is a political act. Once Art is understood, it loses its power. It becomes aesthetic, decorative, pedagogic. Art, thus Artists, must travel over the stepping stones left by the Impressionists, Cubists, by Dada, Surrealism, Anti-Art, Anti-anti-Art, Minimalism, Deconstructivism, the revolutionary movements that have drawn inspiration from communism, anarchy, Buddhism and nihilism, four steps to the void."

Like Jasper Johns, who had taken the Stars and Stripes and painted it, Anton Cesar had recreated our national flag in bank notes. Helena was right: all Art is derivative.

There was a pile of books by designer writers, a stack of credit cards like a pack of playing cards. Spend Spend Spend was the title. In an era of status symbols and gyroscoping recession, the post-modernists with their crushed supermarket trolleys and grey crucifixions had become anachronistic and preposterous.

"...Ah, New York!"

From Cézanne to Cesar, as Cesar liked to say; and he said it often enough for those words to be taken up in print. Self-praise is no praise? How quaint!

The critics had found a message concealed in Anton's work and the grunge in their ears softened to silence the simplicity of his cry: this is what I am. This is what I want. That was why he had abandoned Helena for Sofie.

We collided.

"Madame," he said, bowing, extricating himself from the girls, kissing the back of Ms Ivancheva's toad-skin hand. "You look divine."

"Innovative," she said.

"More daring," trumpeted Sofie with all the self-confidence of a personal trust, a family in brewing.

Helena's brow beneath a feathered hat creased in a way I would come to cherish, the five lines anticipating the intricate notes of an overture.

"There's something I must show you," Anton declared and he took the critic's arm with the air of a palace guard plotting treason. "I love those boots. I have to get a pair. Don't you just love those boots, Sofie?"

"They're *dahling*."

He led the old woman away, gesturing excitedly, Sofie in the slipstream.

I watched with Helena as they vanished into the smoke.

"He's too much," I laughed.

"Much," she said in a serious voice, and I turned to look at her.

"How are you?"

"I'm very well, thank you."

"How's Anton?" I asked her.

"Utterly himself," Helena answered, staring into my eyes, predicting my expression, my pleasure, I suppose.

Her fingers were laced in front of her. Her long oval face was framed by the line of the hat that met in turn the coils of a pink silk scarf, wisps of hair the colour of the light in old amber straying from its folds.

"He always says the right thing and never means it," she added, and I gathered up these words as if they were gifts left below a Christmas tree. There were holes in Anton worthy of Dalí's brush and we would gaze through them together.

Helena was studying me, her head tilted to one side. There were things I wanted to ask but never did. I was on the verge of stammering, the result of my parents' miscalculated guidance, and turned away from her impenetrable blue eyes to stare up at the mannequins. She took my arm, resting her body against mine, a cosy gesture, although I may merely have been a surrogate for her cello. Doubt was in me like a pirate ship in an undefended bay on the Spanish coast. The atonal music had made all conversation expendable and the passing observation seemed momentarily profound as the guests moved through the ghosts of hashish smoke like jinns escaping unstoppered bottles.

I glanced from face to face, old and young, and everyone appeared unfinished, too fat, too short, too tall, distorted, groping, garish, grinning, pointless, humanity *in extremis*. Anton stepped briskly on to a dais. They clapped. He raised his hand for silence, sliding his glasses up his nose, a new affectation.

Bravo. Bravísimo.

The art world had chosen a new king for the day but, like many an author with his lonely opus, Anton had made his statement and would withdraw to the safety of the university where, each autumn, as the leaves were falling from the trees, there came a new flock of sacrificial lambs thirsting for knowledge. He did have his qualities, not as an artist, but a teacher. A doctorate secured his position on the staff. He climbed swiftly into the professor's seat in the studios of fine art and found his place in life, as few men do, on the spiral of learning more and more and more about less and less and less until he knew everything there was to know about the perfumed path that led to the altars of his own insatiable appetites.

"I just have to have them. I have to. I am an explorer in search of Shangri-la, El Dorado, heaven in the here and now. Once you sink into the forbidden garden you possess a woman totally and forever. It is the masculine rite of passage. The idyll prized by the true artist."

He would sigh and refill my glass. His brown eyes had golden flecks like exploding planets. His smile was not the wicked smile of a seaside Punch, but the appreciative smile of the bon vivant. He would tap his temple with his finger.

"The work is all up here. You must concentrate solely on their minds. Never attempt to take a woman to bed. Be patient. Wait for her. Keep waiting and keep filling her thoughts with the joys of the intellect. Give her books, never flowers. Meet on the library steps. Be late. Be irritable and blame Goethe. Have quiet lunches among the workers in the Old Quarter. Take her to Japanese films and let her pay

27

for the tickets. In three weeks you will have her mind and she will be aching to give you all that remains as a token of her gratitude."

Another drink? A cigar, perhaps?

He would resettle himself in a wreath of cushions and, with the expression of a connoisseur with good brandy, would delight in the words of his monologue.

"When they are wet with sweat and the oily juices of their own desire, you turn them over and kiss their shoulder blades. They must have shoulder blades that stick out like the wings of a bird, like fallen angels. Kiss them slowly. Slowly run your lips down their spines. I adore spines. You hesitate at the lair of Kundalini where the snake is beginning to stir, then carry on to the holy orifice with its padlock of pink rose petals, easing it apart. It feels strange but she likes the sensation. The rose opens as if for the sun and, like those sea anemones that trap fish and devour them alive, it draws your extended tongue into the caverns of her repressed fantasies. You must be tender and persistent, like a piston, so that the sphincter, designed to push outward, becomes accustomed to its new role of sucking inward. She starts to move up and down. She never imagined she was going to like it but you have claimed her mind and she loves it, she wants it. Her cheeks open wider and lift into the air like the arms of a child and, at that precise moment, you sink steadily but forcefully in."

Four

I have an erection, as I always did, inapplicable then and inexplicable now in this room awash in silence. Did you turn Helena over? Was she that special one and only one who had orgasms during anal intercourse? If I stand will I see her image behind me in the mirrors? Will I see my own?

It's always been curious to me that so many of us wander the wrong path. Paederasts manage the kindergarten. Racists join the police. Are lawyers honest, in your experience? Or politicians? I'm an architect. The Lion's our leader and Anton Cesar, a teacher of guileless girls, delighted in the benefits of further education. He kept a jar of Vaseline by the bed in his room and, later, in the drawer of his Biedermeier desk.

"Not that it should be necessary. When those smooth round cheeks part like a freshly-ripened fruit, with those slender legs open in a triumphal arch, with her knees pushing down into the bed or the floor or the grass, forcing open that inquiring dark eye so that it looks like the mouth of a fish in a bowl at feeding time, pushing, pushing, up and out. When the dragons that guard the treasure finally pull back from the jaws of the cave they are drenched in desire. They cannot bear the anticipation another second. Fuck me, fuck me, fuck me, they cry, and they want to consume the mystery whole like the devout with their deities..."

He pauses for breath, a sagacious look replacing the awe, his finger running his spectacles back up his nose.

29

"And what if the muscles do tighten, by instinct, perhaps, and in spite of all those lessons in smoky cafés about the struggle for aesthetic harmony beyond the dreary taboos of middle-class morality? Yes, she had whispered, yes. And you apply the vaseline sparingly as you whisper back: I need you, I need you this way. With honesty. As an artist. It's safe. It's natural. It's uniquely human. And in you plunge like a tantric master in sight of the godhead..."

...ah!

Pure pornography?

How predictable! How passé! Allow me to refresh your drink.

Why thank you.

Bottoms up.

"You must remind me to give you a copy of my book on Khajuraho."

Yeah, cheers.

Good health. I drink to find myself in the well of solitude below the antique gilt mirrors. I drink in order to fill those dark cunning tracts we dig over like old men in our back gardens. We are condemned, dear reader, to sow our seed in stony places. What hope is there for us, we who suffer the indignity of serving others less able than ourselves? Did you choose the mazes of the mind over the ciphers of the market? Do you sit in front of the TV set not a computer screen in the converted study? We make one false move - an A in geography - and that's it: the wrong road for life.

It is easier to go wrong than right, going truly wrong by not changing course. Look at all those weary drawn faces of men at bus stops carrying a rolled newspaper home at night and a sandwich wrapped in tinfoil to work each morning. Look at the women, old and alone; abandoned with babies. Me with my briefcase; you with a novel by Milan Kundera.

When opportunity came knocking, why weren't you listening? We were waiting always waiting for a disaster that never came and when it came we weren't prepared for it.

Just as the Moslem hordes cannot have been ready for all the cheerful obscenity they saw when they reached the plains of Khajuraho and found the Hindu temples ornamented so enigmatically with scenes from the Kama Sutra.

After tramping through sloughs of blood, those warriors far from home must have peered like Narcissus into the pool and what they saw was a likeness of their innermost lusts: man, his gods, animals and mythical beasts linked in a divine orgy that is both grand and monolithic: the goatherd taking time off from his goats to stick it to the girl of his fancy; the carpenter engulfed in a dancer's throat, while he gazes open-mouthed at her high, meaty breasts with the stunned look of a schoolboy - *large breasts are like old friends, we want to see them, not be bothered by them*. Confronted by this pious display of debauchery the mullahs unearthed arcane allusions in the Koran and left the carvings to the wiles of destiny.

Is man closer to God when he is inside the female than at any other time?

Professor Cesar poses the question in the text and leaves his reader to find his own answer. How remiss.

My copy of the book is in the study. I had a brief inclination to seek it out but the feeling ebbed like the good intentions of a New Year resolution.

I take my plate, push back the chair and, as I leave the dining room, I become aware of the haunted figures diminishing to infinity among the rows of mirrors. The hall corridor is bathed in the half-darkness, deceiving the eye with ghosts of Helena, Cristian, the makebelieve sister I played with as a child. The kitchen smells of neglect and vegetables, the odour of the workers' quarter. The waste bin, the lid stained, the bottom swimming in an inch of goo, pulses in the corner like a forgotten bomb. I remove the plastic bags when they are full and *M* Erich, the concierge, takes them away. It is not easy scraping the sticky mess from the dinner plate but there's no hurry. I persevere. The plate and silverware find places in the dishwasher I activate every week or so and I return to the dining room to collect the wine. I turn off the lights, conserving energy, a thought which brings the Lion to mind. The more we saved the more we could spend at the Ministry of Architecture.

The study and drawing room are separated by an arch supported by two wooden columns carved from the mast of a wrecked galleon and installed by Helena during one of her excursions into interior design, taking time off from her music, its absence when I returned from the office conferring on the building that air of anticipation that precedes a concert. I hear the cello in the silence and look about me for her shoes, her coat thrown over a chair, the coffee half finished, a book marked with a postcard, sheet music in a pool about the music stand awaiting the maid's guiding hand, as an orchestra waits in discord for the conductor.

She kept herself busy, moving from one thing to the next, changing the rooms, all but Cristian's room. There is so much space in the apartment there was never a need to open that particular door. The past was there with its mocking hopes of coherence and perpetuity, buried with slumbering memories like gardens under snow. On his fifth birthday he rode a bicycle without stabilisers and I was shamelessly proud. It wobbled one way, then the other. I thought he was going to fall but he boldly jerked the handlebars and found a straight course. Two days later, he could ride like the wind, swift and sure, his pale hair flying behind him.

We observed, glowing and afraid. Helena linked her arm with mine. This is what we had achieved. This was our share of the future. We are programmed to remake ourselves in our own image and in our young we look for the qualities life teaches us we do not possess. Mothers ignore the faults of daughters and admire in their sons the very quirks and characteristics they grow to despise in husbands. Life has no point other than reproducing itself. We have nothing more intrinsic to us than a biological function. Even so, dare I say it: Cristian was a beautiful boy and rode his bicycle as if with the winged heels of Mercury.

He had just started school: Emma's a chatterbox; she's always being told off. Pierre wet his pants in class; his mother had to come and take him home. Alex is the best reader and I'm second best. Or third.

We were eating hamburgers. He was colouring a picture the restaurant cleverly provides on the rear of the place mats, inviting us into his world, a society of ingenuous spirits finding their path; looking up at me with Helena's surprised, trusting, sceptical little boy face.

"Can I have another drink?"

What a riddle this question suggests. We want to say yes. Yes. Yes. Yes. Yes to everything. Time is too short for saying no.

"Ask Mummy."

"He asked you," she said.

"You didn't say please."

"Please, Daddy."

"You can this time."

He drinks another drink and she watches as if there is something marvellous in the way his cheeks open and close. It is a mystery to her that he exists at all. She has achieved something meaningful without trying or defeating others. Her eyes have always been vague, her expression unclear. But in Cristian she sees a miracle and glances at me with gratitude.

Like a Hindu wife, the grieving moth has committed suttee on the electric bulb, an oasis of light in the wastes of an indifferent darkness. The mutinous flutes of a Mozart concerto joust against the window panes. In the next apartment, Madame Raimonde and Madame Sorulos are vanishing into the armchairs that stand guard beside an unlit fire.

Four or five (or was it six?) days ago, the widows invited me in and, with all the ceremony of monarchs presenting a decoration, they gave me a lemon, the interest paid on two apples I had given them the week before. They wore the eager, festive expressions of maiden aunts and I stood between them like a boy with a gift he has outgrown. Bending to make myself smaller, we remained rooted to the spot like sunflowers left in a field, three people who meet at a cocktail party and shyly search for something to say. What can you say to old ladies when the weather has been struck from the conversation?

At home, I placed the lemon in the refrigerator where it remains, quite alone, like the stray onion invariably lodged at the bottom of the vegetable box. The past is forever absurd: snapshots, dead grandfathers, broken marriages, childhood.

Do you remember feeling so happy you thought you were going to die from such happiness? Was happiness the picnic meal on a paper plate with a glass of cold beer by the river with friends on a warm afternoon we look back on and know we must have been happy because we can't remember we weren't? I feel like a diver at the end of a diving board who has taken the upward spring and now looks down and sees the pool is empty. While we drank cold beer, there was something creeping up on us like a house cat stalking a magpie. We were Neros fiddling in the flames; men gabbling on about peace while the mines from our factories were blowing out the eyes and blowing off the legs of black people in far away lands. We gabbled on about the environment as the ozone layer retreated and our paper plates took to the wind. Did we destroy our little piece of the earth simply because we couldn't be bothered not to?

We drank cold beer on warm afternoons, berating each other, Anton, Oscar, the playwright, and me; Helena, Sofie and Zoë, who had a Celtic ring tattooed on her thigh, a Red Admiral on her shoulder. We drank cold beer while others were marching, debating our corners while they lay in the streets with their heads cracked open by the long police batons imported from abroad. We were the ones sleeping while others suffered.

I am the rapist who haunts the scene of the crime; the mongrel turning to sniff its own mark on the lamp-post; the wild flower turning to dust between the pages of the arid author's lone novel. I am a man with memories of a coffin so small its sight evoked fresh tears when the time for tears had gone.

I am a man with hands that smell of smoke, a reminder like a knot in a handkerchief of what I should do; of what I should have done long ago. I am a man with dull secrets and empty places, a passive man with flaccid cheeks, tall and bent by digital displays and drawing boards; a water sign who drinks alone in a room clammy with reverie and where the solitary dim light makes a diaphanous stain on the darkness like dried semen on black satin sheets.

Ah, the memory of it all.

We live too long, that's the problem. I cough. I cough more at night. I cough and refill my glass and drink a toast to absolutely nothing.

I am Tomas Sala, state architect. Perhaps you despise me and, yet, we have never met.

Is this self pity?

Do forgive this momentary ramble, this urge to dwell in darkness. I'll turn on the desk lamp and share with you the message from a book I read so many times to Cristian he knew it by heart and yet, with the infallibility of the five year old, always asked the same questions. The book's here somewhere amongst the squalor, behind the jade tree; hideous thing. Finally!

In 1284, the town of Hamelin was suffering a plague of rats. They were multiplying, growing bigger and bolder, fighting the dogs, chasing the cats and biting the babies in their cots. Then, a mysterious stranger in brightly-coloured clothing appeared and offered to rid the town of its vermin for a fee the good burghers consented to pay.

The stranger, whom they called the Pied Piper, played his magic flute in a way that so bewitched the rats they came swarming from their grubby lairs and followed him to the River Weser, where they threw themselves upon the current and drowned.

He returned to collect his reward, only to find the townsmen at a meeting where the aldermen had convinced the others that the sum they had rashly agreed upon was too high and, being honest men, they offered him less.

The Pied Piper knew from experience that all discussion with the elders would be in vain. He saved his breath for his flute, played his enchanting music, and what he removed from the town of Hamelin was the future. The children followed him to the Koppenberg hills where they vanished along secluded trails, never to be seen again. Only the crippled boy was left behind.

"Why?"

"To remind the people what they had lost."

"Why didn't they give the Pied Piper his pocket money?"

"They thought it was too much."

"They said they would."

"They changed their mind."

"I think they're greedy."

Of course, little boy, they were greedy. It is the blind greed of the few that punishes the many. The burgomaster and his xenophobic

37

coterie treated their saviour with the disdain of Pontius Pilate with Jesus, and the man in the street with his church-mouse aspirations and nagging wife raised a clenched fist in group approval. They were unaware and will never learn this facile lesson from natural history: throughout the earth's five continents there exists a species of animal that can change colour to adapt to changing circumstances, a device for self-protection that belongs to that reptile known as the politician. He has a mind span of no more than four years and, like goldfish in a bowl, no memory. He will steal your future. His words are as smooth as Belgian chocolate, so general and fluid they can be shaped like molten steel into anything from a spiral staircase to a rocket hull.

More cash for arms conjures up unspecified threats from unknown enemies, foreigners, Pied Pipers. When they took away the milk from the children the Minister spoke of heart disease and new books. They began to close the hospitals when a government team of fact finders discovered disorders among the workers were psychosomatic, the consequence of sloth. "It's all in the head," the Lion roared, outraged, tapping his red sideburns, leaving gobbets of spit in my ear. When they cut down the trees to put up the Palace he promised to make government more accessible.

The politician, statesman, minister, deputy, councillor, that blue, green, red, orange, hermaphrodite spotted and striped reptile will agree to build a new bridge where there's no river. He will lure out pens to put crosses on the ballot sheet from followers who know without a shred of doubt that every pledge will be broken and still they choose him\her because his\her opponent is no better and it is true what they say, each party is worse than the other.

A politician (partner, son, mechanic, doctor) who sometimes lies and sometimes speaks the truth leaves us not knowing what he\she speaks at any particular moment. You will trust them and they will lie to you and I know you know these things but, listen, I have a dream: I envisage a day when the people flock to the polls just to ruin their papers. When the results are read out by the returning officer we will hear: A - 12 votes; B - 9 votes; C - 2 votes, spoiled papers - 27,191.

What then?

It is only a dream. The converted have no need of sermons. The others have sleep in their eyes, ice in their hearts. You must have seen those withering groupies on election day with blue hair and crumbling bodies poured into polka dot summer frocks. I remember seeing my neighbours last time the Lion called an election hurrying off like two sacks of litter. "We always do our duty and support the League," Madame Raimonde announced, and I had a sneaking suspicion the captain's widow supported the Opposition.

There is nothing more sickening than the sight of senile matrons making goo-goo eyes at politicians. Do not trust old women. Do not trust old men. *Trust me.* I know what I'm talking about. Do not trust anyone who is charming. Charm is a species of dishonesty. And those who seek high office are inherently insincere, avaricious, duplicitous.

I know.

I know them all. I am an adviser, a servant, a bureaucrat. I am a part of them but, whatever Anton Cesar might say, I was never one of them.

Let me explain. I need this mote of indulgence, this naked ear behind the grille of the confessional. It was me, you see, it was me. I was the one. It was my hand that held the pencil that wheeled out the lines that planned Golgotha.

It was me.

I was the one, buried in the onanism of my room, the tap of the headboard like Morse code against the dividing wall. A dab with a Kleenex, a swift gasp of breath, and I'm hurrying to the drawing board adjusting my fly like a drunk bustling back to the bar from the urinal.

I was always there, as steadfast as a birth mark, as loyal as bad breath. I watched with the journalists from a position of safety while the demonstrators spread amorphously over the sidewalk. The earth-movers passed through the park's iron gates, the chain-saws roared and the people pushed forward, placards swaying, banners sagging. A man from the Evergreen Alliance was shrieking something I was unable to make out through a microphone. Some women were crying. A pram toppled over.

The wine opens scars in the memory. I can picture even now the infant in pale pink rolling in the gutter. A screaming mother. Speaker static like a dentist's drill. The crowd spilling on to the road. The police pulling out their long batons and I'm sure I saw more than a few smiles as those uniformed ranks pushed back.

The mounted police appeared, sweeping along Victory Avenue. Some limbs were snapped, blood was shed. It was soon over, the protest like a child wailing for attention in an underfunded orphanage. There were two dozen arrests, one fatality: the baby swaddled in pink.

The park gates were locked and remained locked until the day they were unceremoniously removed like the statues of Lenin, cleaned away like fallen chessmen from the squares of Eastern Europe. The workmen painted wide bands around the trees in a whitewash that stole like fungus to shop windows, the boutiques from the boom years, old family stores, the supermarkets, one after the other. We peered into the green jewel of the parklands, voyeurs and mourners, while the oaks, the elms and sycamores fell. Small boys yelled: Timber. The trees hesitated for a moment, as do the old and lame on the stairs, then toppled with a crash of splintered boughs and shattered branches. Hundreds of years, gone in a flash.

Glints of sunlight slithered like tropical fish over the quivering foliage. Clouds of dust rose into the air, seeming to disappear, only now we know that nothing disappears, but reforms into something harmful that eats its way out into the universe then, like an Old Testament plague, comes pouring back down again. The smell of death mingled with the melancholy doppelgängers of the inner self, the instinctual self that dully recalls something but you're not sure what it is. You must have noticed the shade below a tree is cooler than the shade besides a building? Did no one find time to mention it to the men at the Ministry? Why didn't they go on strike?

Why didn't somebody do something?

Fingers were pointed all too readily at the state architect but he was just a blinkered bureaucrat contemplating Helena's cream meringue; a boy still, unable to distinguish the bond between cause and effect: the harmless doodles on the drawing board and the chain-saws like ravening beasts ripping into the undergrowth.

I'm just a modest man, a mild and middling schizophrenic with voices in his head, imaginary conversations, a singular desire to speak out when there are no ears but your ears to listen:

I'm sorry. I didn't mean it.

41

Five

I have long wondered what people expect of me, of any of us, and now, perhaps, I know: they expect us to leave them alone; leave them in the brittle peace of their petty routines and ignominious pretences. They do not want us to upset the fragile balance of their tabloid lives and lottery appetites. They do not want us to make them think, or see, or feel lost or empty, ineffectual or sad. They want to raise their arms and shake their heads with fleeting sorrow as the chain-saws roar and small boys clap their hands, because they do not know, and why should they know, that when you cut down a tree you are more than cutting down a tree. You erode the soil; tamper with the scenery, the oxygen supply, the habitat of the birds that came to eat our breadcrumbs that day when we drank cold beer and there were others who lay with fractured skulls and broken noses. Didn't Marx say progress would come dripping blood?

There is no purpose to your loathing me. I loathe myself. And, yes, even that is delusion. The swimming pool is a blue cement void below the diving board. It was written in the stars, the lines on my palm, the bumps of my skull, the tea leaves at the bottom of my cup. I was fated, you see, forever fated.

When the First Minister took my computer enhanced drawings away with him from the university twenty years ago (tucked under his strong right arm, as I recall), I was doomed to suckle on the sour milk of early success from which I have never recovered.

I pause to reflect. Bear with me. There is a mystery to solve. It is evolving, weaving its web. You should make yourself some coffee; another glass of wine, perhaps?

Do you sit up late at night with a novel that barely holds the attention and a vague uneasiness like a bothersome fly you are too lazy or reluctant to swat? Do you have a headache at this moment? Or a back ache? Do you feel like crying for no reason? Is it worse in winter? Is suicide an alternative? Is there anything more unsuccessful than an unsuccessful suicide? Life is neither Heaven nor Hell but the limbo of insecurity.

During that pause, I searched among the shelves. I found my original plans for the Palace of Democracy and, yielding to temptation, Anton Cesar's book on Khajuraho.

It opened as if from a curse on a page that shows a goddess being sodomized by a bearded satyr and I returned to my desk with a heavy heart made heavier with the appendaged weight of depression, a recurrent malady that arises from the smallest thing; or nothing: a picture in a book, the look on a stranger's face, the thought of Helena's sister dropping ash down my jacket as she spoke with goo-goo eyes about the Lion.

The depression descends, consumes me utterly, and yet, even while I am wallowing in the gloomy, intolerable depths and believe all and everything is hopeless, I continue to behave in my quiet, impotent way and others are not aware of my distress. By the time I was seven I knew how to hide my feelings, particularly from my parents, who had taught me this discreet craft, mother at the breast, father by his inadequacy and indifference.

They were people who never sunk their teeth into life, allowed the juice to wash over their chins, down their shirt fronts. They lived by a debilitating code: Don't Walk on the Grass. And when you refrain from this luxury you're bound to end up neurotic, in harmony with the age of mass neurosis. Depression is as common to our over populated planet as corruption and all theories put one in mind of the soap bubbles we blew through metal rings as children. They are rainbow-coloured, so exquisite we want to reach for them and, the moment we do, they burst and disappear.

What we are left with is self-analysis, a mad dog chasing its own tail. There are no solutions and the passing salve is as temporary as oil of cloves on a toothache. My mind during depression does not expand but shrinks into a condition where it is only able to focus on the past (Stella's ash on my jacket), as if the days were wet clay that can be reshaped into the various lives I may have led had I been true to myself. I am what I was, what I always was, and always will be. In truth, I have been true to myself, my private anxieties the seeds of a despair that dwell in me like the holiday snaps of people you've forgotten and you can't bear to throw out in case you remember them again.

My method for fighting depression is going to bed and thinking about all the people who are worse off than me: the disabled, blind babies, the starving, AIDS-ridden hordes of Africa, Mimi Sorulos. But the concerns we show the suffering and faceless multitudes merely make one feel powerless, angry, more depressed, more self-concerned. We lay coiled as a foetus between the sheets with thoughts as repetitive as a mantra, making plans like the spokes of a wheel that begin at the same black hub and terminate at the same dead end.

There's never any time to cure depression. Time is taken up by working. We were all working, pressing together in buses and trains, in metros that scream underground, in motor cars that queue in angry columns; streams of cars with our messages of hope: *I'd Rather Be Windsurfing. NO Nuclear Bombs. Save The Whale.* And still the whales are slaughtered for dog meat and haute cuisine by men with a talent for making computers and motor cars. More bombs are made, bigger and better, circling the earth in satellites, protecting us from something and who knows what as we wait for the weekend when the windsurfing sails pattern the lakes in diamonds of red, yellow and blue.

Sunday takes us back from our houses in the hills in a surly ribbon of flashing lights and wailing horns, around the winding roads to the highway, through the maze of tunnels and overpasses to the boulevards of tall, dark buildings where the poor stand in the shadows with outstretched hands and the resignation of congenital migraine.

"It's a disgrace. Somebody should do something," Anton said.

"It's down to the politicians," said Oscar.

"I'm getting out of this country," said Rolf. "The children are healthy. They don't sniff glue. My wife doesn't have affairs."

Your wife does have affairs.

The children do sniff glue. Snort chemicals. Smoke the herbs.

They wear black clothes. Break windows and kick in doors. They steal from your wallet. From their mother's purse. They run in gangs. Running from school. Running from home. Running for drugs. Running for the sake of running and dying mid-step: Aged Fifteen. Sex in the youth club, sex in the street, sex in school and violence everywhere: on silver screens in cinemas, on television screens in

46

living rooms, in newspapers, on news stands, on street corners where men dress as women and women dress like the women they will never be on the pages of periodicals as glossy as the light from an exploding star.

We move along a path like ants in a file seeking identity, individuality, innovation, for ourselves. And everyone looks the same, we wear the same, feel the same, we have the same ideals, morals and desires. We worship the same shallow Braille from the bibles of magazine scribble, eating the same dishes of microwave muck and trying eternally not to open that second bottle of wine. We are all the same; interchangeable. *That* is the zeitgeist. We have stopped being people. We are composites of advertising agency slogans. We are blurb robots and it has taken Mother Irony to find Her own Final Solution: Contamination.

We are killing ourselves. Factories pump out black smog; oil companies leak lagoons of oil and bore into the pristine wilds of Alaska; governments conceal nuclear offal; the hydroponic corporations are sucking the essence from the earth; the chemical industries invest in arms and poison us strategically on land, sea, air and in the temples of our minds as we pop their pills and blindly watch the seams of the world splitting with the patience of great ambition: faceless men with polished shoes and bent shoulders all rushing to work with a sandwich wrapped in tinfoil, and you know what Henry Miller said: you don't have to work for a living. You can always starve to death.

Off we rush to press our flesh against the foetid stranger on the metro and morning train, ad. agency clones, vanishing behind office doors and factory doors, to grease the wheel and turn the wheel and fall beneath the wheel. Overcrowding. Inflation. Recession. Depression. Noise. Another war in the Third World to decorate the columns that pattern the pages around the velvet mount and perfect nipples of the fourteen year old with the candour of Machiavelli. "I'm over the moon," she told our reporter.

How depressing.

If only I had assimilated those lessons from mythology. When the Cyclops peered myopically at the shadows stealing through his cave he demanded Who's there? And Jason modestly replied: It is Nobody.

It is wanting to be more than Nobody that casts us into the pit where we keep digging until we exhume the leaden pot where depression lies. Depression is selfish. There's no argument. Depression is desiring, something you cannot have or do not deserve; desiring to be something you are not and have never been, and never could have been. It is giving in to: pride, covetousness, lust, anger, gluttony, envy and/or sloth, the seven deadly sins passed down to us from mediaeval times and, though amusing for about a millionth of a second, hardly apt for the pessimistic psychoses of the twenty-first century.

Sin itself is as outmoded as the church that invented it and I would like to list an additional collection of human dispositions I have called the Seven Amoral Frailties. I have them here, jotted down in an old diary:

greed
hypocrisy
unconcern

48

vanity

treachery

nostalgia

hope

There are some who maintain that un coeur mélancolique is an intellectual affliction; the man at the plough like the beast that pulls it concerned solely with filling his belly. Camus said an intellectual is someone whose mind watches itself and it could be that it is all this constant watching, weighing up and re-jigging of the past that scratches away the foundations of our everyday well-being to create those murky vacuums where depressions lay their eggs.

The best antidote to depression is sex, preferably with a stranger; better still, a stranger approached at random and with the hope that he or she is likewise a depressive and shares the same need, as an émigré is glad to share his native tongue over the café table with an ideological enemy.

There are a good number of men who play the averages. They may approach a hundred women and get a hundred refusals, a few slaps around the face. But there is always the one hundred and first, the depressive who shrugs and says, 'Why not?' There is no passion in these couplings but it passes the time and it's better than folding the paper and attempting the crossword.

I have tried this distraction myself, infrequently, once with partial success and then, she was not what you could call a beautiful woman.

Helena was staying in Paris with Oscar and Zoë. Cristian had been dead several months and in his memory our bed had remained a serene landscape. I had spent a few hours with Anton and the saga of his latest triumph: just eighteen; a virgin as tight as a *moule;* ribs like the bars of a bird cage; a battle flag of jet black hair, as curly as question marks, as soft as silk; a juicy one. He stroked his beard nostalgically.

We were sharing a bottle of Beaujolais nouveau. Leaves were falling from the surviving trees. The university had been born again in a new shipment of thirsting young minds. He ordered a second bottle. "Not a bad year, considering." He ran his nose over the rim of the glass. His brown eyes were devilishly bright behind half-moon spectacles.

"Four weeks it took me. I'm losing it. Losing it. Four weeks."

He shook his head mournfully; shouted for some bread and cheese; patted his belly, swelling annually; sipped his wine; lit a small cigar, offered the box.

"Thank you."

"I'm a tragic man, Tomas. I am an addict. I am haunted by a spell, a fetish, a *wunderlust.* I must travel over mountains without paths, across seas without maps, over roads without end." He paused to savour the poetry. "The journey is long but anticipation sharpens the appetite." He let out smoke in a long stream for emphasis.

We were in one of the old bars, a narrow, cluttered place with playbills like Chinese ancestors on the walls, barrels piled in pyramids, the echo of Zen koans repeating without answer. Surely it's a rush of air that makes the sound of one hand clapping?

A boy speaking of his plans to make underground movies and a girl just in front of us were holding hands above the table while the

50

boy's free hand dug around in the darkness beneath. "Don't, don't," the girl was saying. "Not here."

I could smell sweat and dampness. Helena was on my mind. Cristian too. It was about the time when I was thinking of giving away his things. It's exhausting looking at dead people's things: shoes worn to a familiar shape, a bicycle, the racing car lamp, secret treasures. I found a cardboard box and inside, held by an elastic band, was a little pile of train tickets and I wondered where they could have come from. We never used public transport.

The cigar smoke was pleasant as it hit the back of my throat. A musician with unwashed hair hooked behind his ears was giving a spirited rendering of something tuneless on the guitar, wrapping himself around his instrument, as Helena gave succour to her cello.

The bread and cheese came. The waiter opened the wine, wiping cork flecks from the bottle neck with an apron unacquainted with the laundry. His name was Georg. He managed a severe smile as Anton slipped a folded bill in his palm.

My companion leaned forward. "One does well being generous to waiters, maids, delivery boys, gardeners and doormen," he declared, lowering his voice. "It's my father's advice. He taught me never to lie, unless it was strictly useful to do so. Never steal, unless a large enough sum were involved. Never explain yourself. And never trust anyone."

I had heard these paternal tributes before, of course. He wanted his father to be someone special, which he was not. And he wanted Georg to remember him, which he did not.

Anton jammed his mouth with bread and cheese, pushed his half-moon glasses back up the ski-slope of his nose.

"An angel," he went on, spitting crumbs. "Worth the effort. She..." He bit off a hanging crust, worked it from side to side, pressing the mixture out from his back teeth, mislaying words, "...like a little rabbit. I thought she was going to kill me. You know what they're like once you get them started."

- *Actually, no I don't.*

He drew on the cigar, took another chunk of bread, puffing, masticating, reminiscing, remembering.

"Helena's still in Paris?" he asked.

"For the time being."

"You must miss her?"

"Yes, I do."

"I've always had a special affection for her, you know. She's an extraordinary woman; courageous, in her way." He broke off to take a sip of wine. "It's a terrible thing. The children are heart broken. I don't imagine they'll ever get over it."

With his own children briefly visiting his mind he topped up the glasses, clinking the lip of mine before he drank, his eyes brightening.

"Just like a bloody rabbit," he continued, nibbling again at the bread.

He was happy. It was a curse seeing his happiness. I had an uncomfortable feeling in my loins and a dreary sequence of thoughts running like a rusty wheel through my head. I glanced at the girl an arm's length away. She had crossed her legs, one foot tucked behind her chair, creamy thighs with a lingering hint of sun tan, red sandals, worn at the heels. I could see fine pale hairs on her shins and bare arms, golden in the white light.

"I turned her over and kissed her shoulder blades. She was writhing with impatience as I slid my tongue down the toggles of her spine. It was perfect: round as a globe, split with a neat seam that opened like a waking eye." He shook his head in wonder. "She was biting my thumb and, I tell you, Tomas, she had the sharpest teeth I've ever come across."

Shrug, bite, chew, exhale, sip of wine.

"No, don't. Not here."

The boy was under her skirt again, steady and slow. When he got home he would rape her and say she'd been asking for it. I imagined her with her clothes torn off. I imagined the rabbit with the bird cage ribs, filling the landscape abandoned by Helena. I imagined all the girls I would never make love to.

Anton went to refill the glasses. I placed my hand over mine. "Have to go," I said.

"Go?"

I stood, stubbed out the cigar. "Someone I have to see. Give my love to Sofie."

"Let's finish the bottle?"

I had turned away. I turned back again. There was something I had always wanted to ask him but the moment wasn't right. "Another time," I said.

I left him with crumbs in his beard.

Six

There was a misty drizzle visible in the lights from the bar. I saw the woman in the distance, approaching slowly below a hat with a wide brim and an orange cape that billowed around her like the sail of a ship bound in flames for Valhalla. She was tall, as tall as Helena, and moved with the ease of the wind.

I wasn't aware that I had come to a halt and was staring at her. She stopped to rearrange her cape, studying me through the gap between her hat and shoulder. We didn't speak. There was no need. She took my arm and led me through the twisting lanes that narrowed as we proceeded into the dark night.

"We shall drink anïs," she said in a voice that was deep and mocking. Her face at that moment, studying me in the ivory haze of the street lamps, contained the mean, inanimate look of a costume mask. She wasn't young. My age, I thought.

"Of course," I replied.

She smiled, seemed less severe. We walked on. The night was subdued. It was the in between time neither late nor early. We were in a place I did not know, a diaspora of architectural survivors as odd as the giant statues of Easter Island. Drug dealers sold hash and heroin in small amounts. The prostitutes were old and gaudy, arms too big for sleeves, cheap as a meal. We passed them, filling doorways, satin dresses stretched like seal skin over swells of slipping flesh. Someone called: "You'd be better off over here, dear."

A man in a floor-length coat hissed. "Coke? Smack?" He was brisk and furtive, a rodent devoured by the shadows.

We stopped at a wooden door. Through a slit, dark eyes were staring out. They peered at me before moving to my companion. When I looked away, I noticed a name carved in the stone lintel: The Wise Monkey. Below, was the single word *Members*.

A bolt was pulled. Inside, it was warm. We wound our way down a curving flight of stairs and entered a passageway. The lights were dim. There were people everywhere, ants in a nest, the laughter and talking oddly distant as if heard from outside a church. Numberless rooms like Russian dolls led from the passage and on into each other. We eased our way through the maze into a vaulted chamber where the woman motioned me to a table beside the bar.

She removed her cape and looked down at me from below the brim of her hat. Her chin projected at an abrupt angle over a long neck. She wore a black shirt, orange tights; hip bones like finger holds on a cliff face, axe sharp. Her breasts were as playful as waves, rising from a still sea, and you want to plunge in, bury your soul in the mystery.

She sat, knees together, feet planted in black boots with silver buckles. I had been thinking about Helena as we walked. Now it was Marten who entered my mind: a long shadow that stretched from the past to this vaulted cellar underground. Instinctively I ran my fingers under my nose. It was still present, the smell of smoke. I had not seen Marten for years but I imagined he was there in the dim lights, in the costume of a prince or Pied Piper. There was a pain in the pit of my stomach, like an ancient war wound that recalls in the mirror all the horrors of war.

A waiter appeared with a frosted bottle and water in a clay carafe. The woman poured. "Anïs," she said, and we drank them down in one. She refilled the glasses and glanced at me with an expression I took for approval.

Organ music occupied the far end of the room. A few couples were dancing. A sallow, completely bald man at the next table was staring at me. I looked away, added water to the second glass of anïs and watched the liquid grow opaque. I looked back at the woman. She had fine tapering fingers with silver rings and orange nails. She sat upright in her chair, as if posing for a portrait, silent, self-possessed, a world on course that had drawn me like a fragment moon into the orbit of a heavenly body. We had hardly spoken but I had a feeling I would tell her things I had never revealed to Helena, to anyone. It is in the small and apparently insignificant details where destiny begins: a phrase, a gesture, a chance meeting, if any meeting is merely chance.

"I am Pandora," she said, her voice rich, dark with meaning, slightly foreign.

"Tomas."

"Do you know who I am?" She opened her eyes wider to tell me. "I am the one who upset the apple cart." She leaned forward and, for a moment, resembled Anton Cesar. "Beware of envy. Beware of judgments."

The man at the next table pulled his chair closer and finished the anïs in my glass. Pandora kissed his bald head, leaving a mark. She took a compact from her bag and redrew her lips, gazing into the mirror with a detached expression, as if she were painting the lips of another. The man continued to scrutinize me with eccentric absorption, then lost interest. He was nursing a fez, stroking it occasionally like a cat. He had a fine moustache cut in a chevron across his top lip, curdled eyes that seemed to move with erratic independence as he fished around in the pockets of his robe. When they focused, the act coincided with his success in locating a small wooden box which he produced, sliding back the lid. He took out a cone-shaped joint, lit it, took the smoke deep into his lungs and passed the joint to Pandora, who did the same. She gave it to me. I inhaled the smoke. The pain had gone. It was as if a long cord had been wrapped around my neck, then ripped away so that my brain span like a spinning top.

"Buddha sticks with Manali," the man said professionally.

He talked on: the hashish used by the devotees at the Shiva temples throughout India is taken from plants that grow in a certain valley in Manali, high in the mountains. They extract the resin at sunrise. The crop is blessed by a priest. It is caked in bricks, wrapped in hand-made paper and sealed in wax.

My concentration had wandered. I took another pull on the joint and, passing it back to the Turk, he held it aloft like a trophy.

"So soft, the softest you can find; soft, brown, patterned with lights of gold," he said in the tone of a housewife with a new cake mix, elation ranging over his Himalayan features.

He turned to me. "They use Manali in New Zealand to help cancer patients. It makes them feel good," he cried, slapping his palm on the table top so that it rocked and spilled the drinks.

The Turk stood. "Please," he said, handing me the fez.

He took Pandora's hand and escorted her to the dance floor. A man at a synthesizer played circus music. He had masses of smoke-stained hair and a face once handsome now sagging like the bellies of the prostitutes in the street outside. Pandora led the dance, holding her partner in such a way that his bald head was buried below her breasts.

57

I had the feeling I was in an ancient catacomb of Arabic design, a riddle of passageways connected by concealed doorways leading to forbidden places Anton Cesar would have left or never entered. The smoke swirling about the arched ceiling was multi-coloured and through it the bar's habitués had the appearance of performers in tableau vivant. Most were men. A number of the women were men also although there were some obvious exceptions.

Close to me, perched on a stool like an item in a store, was a girl with restless skinny legs she kept crossing and uncrossing like a pair of knitting needles. She had the eyes of a newly hatched bird and a pink tongue that caressed lips shaped in a bow of the kind a faun might carry. Her hair was a pleat with golden strands hanging so coyly about her brow and bare shoulders one could only appreciate the artifice. She was Anton's ideal: the daughter who arouses dreams of incest. Her name was Baby.

How's it been, Baby?

Like the boots, Baby.

Want a drink, Baby?

She was laughing with everyone who passed, skinny pimps in ear-rings that promised eternal youth; swashbuckling machos with mad eyes and Stalin moustaches; the magistrate with a secret life. No one bothered her. She was a part of something; a Member.

The musician played on, the room swaying just faintly from side to side, as if it were the deck of a ship. I finished the glass in front of me and poured a third. Or was it a fourth? I am confused by numbers and dates. I forget when Cristian was born and when he died. It was over quickly. He had a stomach ache, a headache, a high fever that

58

hollowed his eyes and slashed deep lines on his seraphim face. The doctor remarked fatuously that he had been brave.

I looked down at him, tiny below the white bed cover. I would willingly have changed places. Death is the affair of the living, the ones left behind. Memories hang about me like unfinished business. Time measures the universe by beginnings and endings. The middle is a vacuum where a voice calls in sleepless hours between creased damp sheets, the morning light pressing against the dawn. I hear the voice when others speak and what they say becomes trite and incomprehensible, a single sound that repeats like an echo:

"Daddy, Daddy."

It is the name of destiny. I say this little word and I'm sober. There are tears in my eyes. They are a comfort. We should have shed more tears. A river of tears. Enough tears to float the basket of our suffering so that it sailed away on the mournful tide and disappeared.

Now that he's gone, the theme, the plot, the very design has unravelled. Our sole function is to continue the line, like the birds, the rats, the zebras. Like the spider that is only one tenth the size of its blind female and must avoid her poisonous embrace, even while mating. This undertaking, far from creating apathy, inspires a Trojan subterfuge: he brings the gift of a dead fly to her web and, as she greedily wraps it in silk, he nips in for a hasty poke. That little spider wants sons and is willing to risk his life to get them. Babies will eat their own dead mothers to survive and have more babies that will succumb like Cristian to unknown diseases.

"The air killed him," said Oscar, the playwright, whose plays on pollution were never performed. He had joined the Evergreen Alliance after they cut down the trees, then left for Paris with Zoë, continuing

59

the fight in exile without heeding Trotsky's counsel that all revolution starts from within.

All I know is that my baby's lungs stopped pumping and I carried the box we buried him in on an autumn day below black clouds and it weighed no more than a briefcase. Helena stood at my side, a portrait by Francis Bacon. Her immobile features made me think of an obscure talisman carved from the seas of wax in an ancient cathedral; her eyes the agonized blue of a costly German car: subtle, unaligned eyes that correct the tilt of the world by the permanent tilt of her head. Even in our wedding photographs Helena was looking at me sideways as if she suspected my seed would betray in Cristian a pulmonary weakness.

She fled to her cello. She sat in the bay beside the tall windows, the amber glow of her hair lighting her narrow face as she bowed the strings with the fierce energy of a drowning swimmer, the deep, rounded, tormented notes reverberating about her in one sheet of turbulent sound. Ah but to have recorded those days of unpredictable euphony! The instrument had become a part of her and as I watched they were as lovers at the height of a terrible passion. The tone was emotional, yet delicate and sonorous, a domed empty space she coloured with contrasting shades, foreboding during the opening theme of Brahms's E minor Sonata, and we were standing side by side before a tiny grave; impassioned by Beethoven's Opus 69, and I want to take her in my arms and search for the light that has died in her marble eyes. In the last movement of Dvorak, there is a flash of gaiety, as even in depression there are moments of respite, but she is distant once more for the slow, wistful nucleus of the Lalo.

She does not speak or eat. She plays music. The neighbours stand in open doorways listening. They do not complain. On the contrary. They have been transported to the shores of their own most intimate fears, all death a reminder of the fragility of us all, the cruel impermanence of ice separating on a lake, of fire consuming a barn. They wear pastoral smiles, lowering their heads as their eyes meet mine. Alun and Sylvie no longer ran screaming through the halls. Their broken hearts are still in pieces and they sit in corners eating chocolate bars, each square laying a path to that far away place of their healing. Sofie asks if there is anything she can do. She worries that Helena is growing too thin and would like to be too thin herself. A death mask is forcing its way through Helena's papyrus flesh, the five lines marking her brow so sharply I wait each day for the brand of a treble clef.

I make her eat. She obeys like a child, chewing rice like it's an elastic band she has in her mouth, sipping milk before I put her to bed and in bed she wraps herself about me, climbing into my enfolding arms as if I am a leather case lined in faded blue velvet. She sleeps naked as always and I stroke her fine thin body and it is like running my palm over the wooden curves of the cello. I feel her frail breath on my neck. It is in honour of Cristian that we do not make love. I hold her. She sleeps. I lay awake and listen to the hushed prayer of the night. She stands in the doorway wrapped in a sheet as I leave for the office and by the time I descend the stairs and exit from the main door of the building I can hear Elgar's Cello Concerto in E minor Opus 85 through the tall bay windows. For six months she played the cello and in the seventh she packed her bags and followed the exodus to Paris, leaving a note to say she would be back. She didn't say when.

I finished the drink in my glass and refilled it. The girl on the stool laughed, throwing back her shoulders. Our eyes met for a moment. She smiled, and I looked away.

The bald man had disappeared with sudden urgency. Pandora returned to the table. Once more she stood above me so I could admire her; smell her. She blew an extravagant kiss to the girl.

"Isn't she delicious?"

"Yes."

"Do you want her?"

"Of course."

"It is one of life's fondest jokes. We desire most what we cannot have."

Pandora stared at me with a look I found hard to interpret. I thought she liked me. At least, I think that was what I thought. Even our thoughts are an enigma. We chose one life ever fearing another may have been better. May have been possible.

She smiled for just a second. "Perhaps you will. One day," she said.

"Perhaps."

"And when you do it will be too late."

She glanced at Baby. I lit a cigarette. I used to enjoy smoking, before the cough. It gives you something to do with your hands. I liked the ritual: breaking the cellophane, snapping open the lid, pulling out the silver paper, offering the packet. I would play with the matches, lighting them, one after the other, observing the flames, burning my fingers.

I drew smoke into my lungs. I could see my reflection in the mirror behind the bar. It was someone whose name I was unable to remember and whose face I could scarcely recall, a stranger with thinning hair and drawn cheeks, wild eyes without colour. I must have been about thirty-five then and I'm older now, a winded athlete chasing the years over a muddy incline.

Baby's legs were wide apart. She was wearing poor little match girl boots with laces, clumpy yet congruous with a white party dress tied at the back with a bow.

"It is strange weather we're having," Pandora said, as people said.

I put water in my glass.

"You are an artist," she continued, a statement, not a question. "You have that look about you. Artists are absolute beings with fire behind their eyes, or they are so empty you see only seas of ash. In the last layer of Hell, Dante places ice not fire, silence, not flames. Fire changes. Death is eternal."

"I am an architect," I said.

"I know who you are."

She became quiet.

Everyone knows who I am. Everyone but me.

We drank the last of the anïs. My head was still astray somewhere but the drink brought everything into focus.

"You have something you wish to tell me?" she asked.

"Not now," I answered.

She stood, swung her cape around her shoulders like a matador. "Come."

She paused at the bar to kiss the girl, holding her cheeks between her palms and pressing down with her lips.

The waiter gave me a bill, which I paid.

The mist had gone. The street had grown milky with starlight. Pandora walked in bold strides, like Helena. We saw no one. The buildings grew taller. The street lamps disappeared and I was glad of the starshine, a carpet bringing me to some place alien.

"Come," she had said, come with me to another galaxy. The moon was a silver crescent, fine as a sword, close enough to burn.

If you see the moon through trees you will be struck by a spell, Marten had once said. But there were no trees now. We were safe.

I followed Pandora through a door and up an iron staircase. Her footsteps made a tapping sound like raindrops on a window. The stairs came to an end at a spacious loft infused with the bouquet of frankincense. It was not a living room for living in but being in: a being room without tables or chairs, ashtrays or bibelots, a room where you left your former self at the door and entered to kneel like a convert before the idols of a new religion.

The ceiling was way above, a mosaic of glass, black as sky. The walls were concealed by hanging drapes in silk and satin, in hues of red, copper and gold; brocades, kilims, jousting pennants, flying carpets suspended on silver wires. They moved almost imperceptibly on the currents of hidden breezes, ghost winds, shimmering mirages that strayed among the shadows. I thought I saw Anton and Sofie. I was certain I saw Helena. My wife had grown older, thinner, more distant. There were lines at the corners of her mouth, two deep creases between her eyes. She appeared listless, anxious, a prey to obsessions. How greatly we imagine we know each other and how little we do.

Were we happy together? Had we ever been happy, truly happy? Did our marriage have substance beyond habit, a solitude shared? Now that Cristian was dead, should we make another one?

The incense was numbing. My head was a Chinese puzzle, a complex of wooden shapes that fit together to make a perfect sphere, or don't. I heard music approaching from beyond the moving strips of silk and satin. A cello, naturally, bruised and alone. The anïs was scraping holes from the soft places behind my eyes.

Pandora was slowly unbuttoning her shirt. It slipped to the floor and she stood in the reflection of a triptych mirror where her study was a critical examination, not at all vain; more clinical.

"You have wonderful breasts."

She paused, staring at me over one shoulder, lifting her eyebrows.

She stepped out of her boots and tights, still analyzing her image in the glass, front and back. The music was sombre like ocean waves at night, rhythmic and invisible. She was wearing pink pants cut high at the sides, lengthening her long legs. She kept them on. She removed her hat. She had milky skin and pale orange hair cut boyishly short.

"You're beautiful," I said.

"Is that important?"

"We have made it so."

She opened a window and a draught fingered the drapery, the veils parting to reveal cushions scattered in piles like rocks on the sand. There was a brass bed with black sheets, two metres across, two metres long. Behind it were numerous photographs of Pandora, all square, miniature reflections of the bed, too small to study until I drew closer.

She was posing in the formal, faintly irritated way of the fashion model, displaying her breasts with disdain, turning to show a sinewy bottom, and turning again to expose something I had not been expecting although perhaps I had. It was a penis, coiled like a sea urchin between her thighs.

She had moved behind me. Her hands played over my hips and into my trousers. My head was spinning, swimming, just slowly, in time to the music. My clothes fell away and I came to rest on the big bed like a wrecked ship on the sands of shifting time. I was very tired.

Like a boy taking a drink from a lake, cupping his hands and lifting the water to his lips, Pandora took me into her mouth and, thinking of Baby, I shed my seed in the barren soil of her warm and tender throat. She snuggled me down and I slept where I most wanted to be, pillowed on the miracle of her flawless breasts, as real as the promises of hope and happiness, dreaming dreams of diving boards and dark blue voids, of Marten and the white house, smoke swirls about my fingers, a memory as old as childhood. It is to you that I drink, Pandora, the best friend I ever had. Man or woman.

Seven

It is now about the time when I would normally drop my bones in bed but this night I am content with my wine and clippings, odd thoughts in the margins of magazine pages like voices whispering from another dimension. The drawers are bottomless wells of lost quotations, shabby diaries, Post-its with notes reminding me of things long forgotten. It is a catharsis. I am expunging something; cleaning out the attic; throwing away the memorabilia; raising up the dust of dissipated time: hanging out the dirty linen. I am reaching a decision without ruminating on anything explicit. The mind has its own mind. When we are unable to think of a word we concentrate on something else and the brain tosses it out like a credit card from a bank wall.

It's like that. A decision is breaking from its mould like a butterfly from a chrysalis and some surviving instinct warns me that it must appear without the breath of warming air that would urge it on its way.

It is one of the advantages of nascent middle age: and, believe me, there's not a lot. We grow more patient as well as impatient. The extremes are greater. The memory is stronger as well as debilitated. I am a Pisces (did I say?) born in the cycle of those myopic fishes swimming constantly in opposite directions like former lovers who pass in the night. My feet are pigeon-toed and turn in so far I have always been just as certain of the path going one way as that going the other and have thus remained here in this dying city of procrastinating strangers, the hapless, hopeless and has beens, the mesdames widows crouching behind the crumbling citadels of their own petty nostalgia, a million of us where once there were many millions, clinging on with the rats, the pigeons, the spent air that smells of sulphur, the acid rain that takes the gloss from cars, the paint from the woodwork, the stripes from the dirty linen. Decisions come slowly, awkwardly. I am deciding something about something. It doesn't matter what, for it has put me in good spirits.

The depression has lifted. I'm in the reposed and pacified mood that settled about me as a student immersed in work, my pencil guided subliminally, building illusions, going places my conscious mind would never have reached. My drafts became plans, then printouts, and it is those printouts here in front of me that are seminal to everything that was to follow: the honours and criticism, the offensive phone calls, even Helena. I would listen to the headboard tapping against the wall as Anton relieved another virgin of her onerous gifts and, as my imagination followed like a porter with the bags, a hard on like a vaulting pole would muscle its way into my palm. The sound waves of other people's sex is disconcerting yet intoxicating. The tapping would gain in momentum, climbing towards a drum roll, my grip tightening like strangler's hands around the neck of a child until I exploded in harmony with the inescapable crescendo, a muffled scream in staccato exhaled from the back of the throat, a messy finale wiped away with a Kleenex before I returned to the plans, my body dry as a mummy, as hollow as the feeling that ensues when waking with a hangover, something we do every day. The headboard would start again, gently now, as Anton turned them over and kissed their shoulder blades, the sound muted, as far away as the silence across the balcony.

I have this fragment of memory as sparkling as a copper coin cleaned in Coca Cola. I can see us now, Pandora, Baby and me, the three of us sitting around a table in a bar, the rain swishing against the window, the ashtray full, my fingers avidly turning a cigarette box into a silver spider. Helena had returned from Paris, only to leave again. It was easier being an exile. She liked the light over the Seine, the smell of baguettes, the girls with boys' faces, mirror images of herself. All is vanity. The Palace was complete, although the complex rolled on like a dust storm, a hurricane. There were people out there in the clammy grey streets who wanted to do me harm and who can blame them. Christmas was coming and, as it is for many of us, it was a time for despair.

Baby was wearing skin-tight tights and a sweater demanding constant readjustment as it slithered snake-like from her shoulder. Her hair was neither up nor down. Her lips were the pink of tropical fish, never quite closed. She smoked and I smoked and Pandora talked in her dark voice and it would have been bliss to have remained seated forever at that table in that bar with the rain streaking the windows.

We don't appreciate those glimpses of paradise until they have gone, just as Baby did not appreciate the lilliputian nub of perfection the fates had granted her. She was hauling her sweater tirelessly back into place, while I watched it slide off again, while Pandora constructed a universe from the hair, skin, tissue, muscles, blood, veins, juices and jism between Baby's legs. It is a treasure, a palace, a whip. Before you share it men are dogs yelping for a collar and leash. Let them yelp. Drive them wild. Practice patience. When he finds the courage and suggests meeting drive him wild by saying yes, hesitating, then no.

"...Friday, how awful, I can't. I'm going to an opening."

He won't ask what it is that's opening. That wayward yes is a flame licking the dead wood of his rash optimism. There is something distinctly, unforgivably bourgeois in making dates; something impalpably vulgar. Arrangements must be understood, inevitable, effects sparked by negligent causes. Anything manufactured is automatically suspect and not to be trusted, as the middle-classes can never be trusted.

Next time he tries, as he will, say you must accompany an aged aunt to a gallery. "She's quite mad but irresistible," tell him. "A veritable anarchist." Listen for the polite laugh and interrupt. "I guess she was rather daring in her day, famous, infamous. She did things with Dalí. Or was it the Dalai Lama? She danced naked in New York. Such a scandal."

Tell him Mateo is starring in a play and he's your very oldest, best friend. "I'd simply love you to come but I don't have a ticket myself. Not exactly." Tell him about Marc, your most favourite friend in all the world, more than Matt, even. "He's really fantastic and now he's in hospital after a ghastly motor bike crash. Just like James Dean. It wasn't even Marc's fault." Tell him you have to help Luc choose a gift for Marie and you've known Luc for absolutely forever. Longer than Marc, even. "You must meet Luc. He's a crazy boy. You'd just love him. I do." Tell him Jon's visiting for a few days before going on tour to the Balkans with his rock band.

"Sort of super-highway garage pulp. But cute."

He'll call again. And again. And if and when you do agree to meet, go to a restaurant, never a cinema or theatre. You glow in candlelight. Order dishes from every course, push the food around

70

your plate and eat nothing. Your mama may have apoplexy. He'll find it adorable. Talk excitedly about your disciples: Matt's reviews, Marc's progress, Luc has broken up with Marie poor Marie and Jonny and the Virus have released an album: "Scratch on the Tracks," say. "Weird. But cute."

Have a friend call on the mobile while you're eating and talk rapidly in a confidential, wide-eyed way. Have him/her call back thirty minutes later. Don't explain, don't apologise and, if he asks who it is, which he won't, say it's the eccentric aunt calling from abroad.

"She's sort of special."

So are you. Be disagreeable. Tell him the person you would most liked to have been is Che Guevara. Maybe Imelda Marcos. She did so much for women. Show a hint of palpitating breasts, a naked stomach flat as an eight-ball table, ringed in silver. Do not giggle. Choose unmatching clothes. Wear the shortest skirt indecency provides and when it rides up, never, never shuffle it down. Be in a hurry. When alone, be self-absorbed. Do not look at other people in bars and cafés; read a book, not a magazine. Do not fear: the men will be looking at you and the girls will be looking at the men looking at you. Bite your lips. It makes them swell. Men look at legs, then lips. How odd that we find so much joy quaffing another's bodily fluids, spending hours during the first bubbling gush of romance sucking a damp organ that returns a pleasure more abstract than rational.

This game young girls play is oh so brief, a few years and, like sand sifting through an hour glass, it trickles to nothing. Men want to take that maidenly membrane and nail it to the mast of their manly craft. No quest is greater. No mountain higher. No deity more divine. It is the summit of success; the inherent and hidden principle of all things: the face of God smiling. There is nothing like a virgin. Men will pay. Mortgage their home. Sell their child. Sacrifice a good marriage. They will give ten years from the end of their life. Fall to their knees and genuflect to the oily orifice, that bundle of tricks, the little miracle, the masterpiece, that obscure object of desire, as Luis Buñuel so adequately put it. They will go to prison. Go into exile. Go mad. In the space age it's the space that matters most. Politicians don't give a wank about war, famine, the trees disappearing, rivers filling with faecal streptococci. Power's the ultimate aphrodisiac and all that power's going into poking their pens in the ink wells of ambitious secretaries, friend's wives, constituents. Hell's Angels hang used condoms on their belts, as Indian braves once displayed bloody scalps as prizes. Men want notches on the gun. Anecdotes for the bar. Soiled triangles of silk as mementoes in the bottom drawer. There is no question of our having to come to terms with our limitations, only our hypocrisy. How many times have you castigated others for the crimes you subliminally want to commit? How do we manage to live with ourselves?

I'll tell you how; Pandora knew how: *we are forced to live with ourselves because no one else will have us.*

Her words and thoughts are so entangled with my own I don't remember who said what. She's gone now; they've all gone. Yet I see her features in my mind's eye like the snap shot of Cristian creasing in my wallet. How special she was. How wise. She knew everything there was to know about being a beautiful woman and yet, for all her courage, she never found the nerve to recast her accoutrements with the final snip & tuck.

The radio is still. The moths no more. The lamp casts oblique reflections. The widows have retired, saying good night in bird chirpy voices before entering their rooms, one pink and chintzy with yellowing photographs of a captain deceased five decades; the other awash in wardrobes and chests like famished whales in underwater nightmares; brown carpet, dead paintwork, a sagging bed like a waterlogged trawler. When did Madame the colonel's widow last share that sunken vessel?

There is an inch of wine at the bottom of the bottle. Silence outside the shuttered windows. The night is black like animal fur without stars or vagrant moon. The Palace plans are folded in leather bindings. All that belongs to the past turns to dust. Earth unto earth. Ashes to ashes. Life is a road that vanishes behind us, crumbling away with each new step. The dewy sweet bloom of youth lasts but a moment. Girls do not gradually grow into women. It happens the first time they see a man looking at them and understand what it is he's looking for. It blossoms at fourteen or thirteen. At twenty-three the smell's delicious. By twenty-eight, tenderness already tends to the overripe: the pungent process of decay has begun. There is nothing more delectable than a coy virgin; nothing more sickly than a matron playing the débutante. You are encumbered, each girl at birth, with a magic gift and magic like love swiftly fades to repetition and fear. Fear of the unknown. Fear of being alone. Fear of being caught. Fear of opening a door and catching your partner partnered with another.

The day he looks distant and vague, saying "Of course, dear," without listening or hearing you know there are fresh flowers he wants to pluck. What awaits: ennui; flash rows or, worse, courtesy;

mechanical sex, rolling to the edges of the bed as if a frontier of rusty cans marks the centre. Where now is joy and purpose? Sylvie's A in geography. Alun a runner-up in the golf tournament. Their smile is your happiness and your task is all but complete.

Forgive me, Anton, the names are mere illustration. How are the twins? Has Alun cultivated a beard like his dad; or does the moustache suffice? What progress with Sylvie's *regimen?* How proud you must be with the nose and broad shoulders she borrowed from you, the rugby prop legs, that wealth of dark hair. How clever you were, finding time to send your stuff into the future, your own self remade in varieties of both sexes. Does Alun employ the mystic fingers of his father's tailor? Will Sylvie fuck Uncle Michel? Sofie did. Will they come and share the long, dormant hours of twilight?

Rest assured. Gold's as good as gold; better than God. Sofie's stack is prodigious; a paper pile in a far away place. They write about it in women's magazines, figures embraced politely by parenthesis.

They are different.

The rich understand the meaning of life and donate readily to the church, mosque, synagogue to ensure the meaning is never revealed. They arrive for prayer wearing large hats and stand like wolves among the sheep staring serenely into the void while the good shepherd, mullah, rabbi, necromancer spins out parables of poverty, humility, giving, sharing, shutting up and turning the other cheek. It's easier for a camel to pass through the eye of a needle than a rich man to enter the kingdom of God. Well, of course. The kingdom of God doesn't exist except as a pile of precisely cut blocks holding up more blocks and smaller blocks until the pyramid reaches the golden capstone where people live golden lives in a state of grace and perfect harmony.

They grappled like Gandhi our good mums and dads with the eternal fantasy: equality, and we live with their remarkable achievement. The workers and middle-classes have turned to crime, just like the well-born and better off, morals shifting from anachronism, as Hitler put it, to irrelevance. Life's very meaning has grown inextricably as one with the quiz show, bingo, pools, the scratch card and lottery; in nothing more than money: Spondulics. Shekels. Brass. Bread. Lucre. Lolly. 'ackers. The oof. The Oodle. The dosh. Bonds. Stocks. Shares. Cold Hard Cash. Yes, that's what we want. Lovely stuff, innit! Light yer cigars wivit. Paper the walls wivit. Lay it on the floor and fuck the missus onit. Tell the neighbours where to stickit 'cos you've gotit and they're up the whatsit without a you know what.

It's those oiks again, out of the markets and into the market!

Money.

Those with it buy the best and imagine they've been blessed with taste. They have more confidence and - now here's a funny thing: they're *nicer*, more industrious, considerate, conscientious, kind. They send thank you notes. Truman Capote said they serve smaller vegetables. And people who have always had money are *even* nicer than those who have acquired it along the way. The children of the rich are forever on the phone, constantly in attendance with their good manners and open palms; they love their parents with a deep and passionate love the poor are too poor and vulgar and boorish to appreciate or comprehend.

Sylvie will find a husband, you can be certain, with all that hair. And Alun is hardly what you would call fat; hardly. "He has a healthy and high regard for food," you remarked in all seriousness that day across the anniversary table, pushing your glasses up over the bridge of your nose, watching the boy's lips move as he read the menu to himself.

The fat love food. When they're not eating they're thinking about what they're going to eat, visualising dishes piled with tantalising treats, bubbling, boiling, baking, steaming, simmering in cauldrons, browning under the grill, roasting in ovens, freezing in the fridge. Alun's eyes and Sylvie's eyes, like two pairs of dancers, fox-trotted the nearby tables, studying the ravished plates with the scientist's regard for a rat's liver crawling with cancer; hesitating with approval, hurrying on over the yoghurt and piss green cups of jasmine tea. They notice the perfume of the food; the blend of spices. A little too much basil. Perhaps a dash more marjoram? Is it well done or overdone? Rare or underdone? They smack their lips and lick their chops and bite their tongues in anxious anticipation. They are vivisectionists dissecting with infinite precision; peeling, prodding, poking and pushing; squeezing and teasing that last slender sliver of transparent flesh from the knotty peak of the crab's claw; herding like a sheep dog stray peas awash in the gravy.

We tried conversation but they are well-behaved children, consumed in their solemn proclivity, cutting their food into neat pieces and chewing thoroughly, thoughtfully, making each morsel a meditation like a Buddhist monk with a grain of rice (like Helena eating elastic bands), lining up the next mouthful in rhythmic strokes.

76

They eat with composure, with dedication, setting out like long distance ramblers to reach the destination of an empty platter.

I studied them surreptitiously when they had finished, sitting back, a little lost, fingers twitching. Thumbs circling. There is a hint of disappointment in those button bright eyes as they wait with a traveller's air of false patience, concerning themselves with the orderliness of the unoccupied cutlery, the location of the salt and pepper pots, the exact positioning of the plate, pushing it away and pulling it back again for a final check.

Another mousse?

Ooo, yes please.

I would like to be a fat man, they seem so jolly sitting on bar stools nursing the dolphin swimming over their belts. They laugh more, fat men; drink more, smoke more, eat more, of course. Fat little boys are sad little boys teased by bean-pole chums and fat little girls grow fatter consuming bile with every creamy sweet nibble. Have you noticed fat girls always wear big ear-rings? They roam the aisles of department stores and whatever they choose, however much they pay, they resemble potato sacks sprouting limbs of smoked ham with piggy features in faces scowling from puddings of raspberry ripple flesh. Do not trust fat women. Fat is an indication of greed, the first of the Seven Amoral Frailties, self-inflicted, an addiction. Why is it the rich stay thin and the poor inflate? Look at Sofie. Look at Anton. Have you ever sat next to a fat person in an aeroplane? Or a theatre? Fatties are gladiators for the forces of ignorance. Disregard their mumbles about glands, big bones. "I have an eating disorder!" There are few fat people in the Sudan and the fat few are in politics. Or police administration. Or the World Bank. There is only one way to lose weight. Forget exercise, massage, prayer. If you have to put something in your mouth, take the example of the stone dancers on the temple walls of Khajuraho.

It has just occurred to me that the hungry ache in my innards is due to hunger. There is nothing to eat in the apartment but a lonely lemon, a phantom onion, the microwave meals for one. Every night it's the same. Melancholy passes to random anger at the end of the bottle and I stare at the dregs in my glass toying with thoughts of opening another. One I can manage. A second will alienate tomorrow and tomorrow the fruits of decision may ripen and fall from the tree.

It is ten o'clock. It seems later. It always seems later. The hours are mercilessly slow individually, accumulatively fast. This day has been endless. My life short. Just a breath and we're gone. The memory is a spiteful mistress moulding events with imprecise hands. We wander in a past reshaped or a future swaddled in victory, the fleeting moment passing without our appreciating its significance.

I should apologise. I am not a Fatist. If you are fat, enjoy it. It's relative. Anorectics imagine they are fat. Bulimics fear it. On some those pounds sit favourably like ornaments. Indian women grow plump to show the wherewithal of their husbands, dressing in saris with a naked midriff where all that wealth can pout like a lascivious lip over their skirt band. Oh to have been a Chinese sage. The *Tao Te Ching* was once my gospel. Helena and I would read a few verses aloud to each other in bed before we made love: by removing bricks from a wall to insert windows we discover profit from what is there, usefulness from what is not there.

The space, the gap, the hole is undervalued; misunderstood. The hole is essential to the needle, the doughnut, the lock on the self-closing door that needs no bolt. While we search through the valleys and crevices of woman, it is the crack, the split, the slit, the hole we wish to find. Shakespeare paid homage to the pause. De Chirico the space. The general the gap in the enemy's defences. John Lennon tells us there are four thousand holes in Blackburn, Lancashire; rather small, all accounted for. There are tunnels running through the earth where legends dwell. From wells we draw water. We drill holes for oil and gas, essential to our well-being and destruction. There are holes in the ozone layer that allow the darkness in. It is the cracked - bless them - for it is they who let in the light. Lao-tsu sees the space between earth and heaven as a bellows. The shape changes, not the form. The more it moves, the more it yields. Remove the surroundings from a hole and there is nothing. From nothing comes nothing. I wish I were fat. I am getting thinner, wasting away, vanishing into that point at the end of an avenue of trees in a painting. I always assumed there was some perfect life and it needed just the right turn in the labyrinth and I could have entered the group, become a Member. The corpulent have their club. So does Pandora. And Helena; exclusive, confidential.

I share my sorrows with my memories so you will see how much greater are mine than your own. You, yes you: you depressive, you misanthrope, sitting there in the half light with your empty bottle and an aching nostalgia for the good ol' days long ago when you were sixteen surrounded by the best friends the world has ever known or will know or could know. You complain when you've nothing to complain about. There's food in the fridge. Coffee in the cupboard. Books on the shelf.

You are the apogee of the homo sapien. You, yes you. You with your central heating and air conditioning; instant food and bottled water. You are the beneficiaries of the agricultural revolution, industrial revolution, a world war, another world war, lots of little wars, welfare, Microsoft, e-mail and the mobile phone. You have seen other lands, how other people live, things of which your grandfathers would never have dreamed. You are surrounded by electronic devices that would've made Einstein's eyes pop. There're late night movies on the television. You have magazines, newspapers, radio stations, information and news in a downpour, a torrent, a landslide. You can fish the deeps of the internet; surf the superhighway. You have your finger on the pulse of the universe.

So, you didn't get the pay rise you expected. The girlfriend stood you up. The wife walked out. Your life is a luke warm bath growing steadily colder but let me tell you something: you're not alone. If you imagine you're special you're doomed. Look in the mirror, comrade. Look in the mirror and ask yourself this question:

Does it really matter?

When you've got them you don't want them and when you want them they're hard to find. Stop thinking about yourself, picking over the past; teasing the scab from all those disappointments and poking your fingers into the soft and seething sore. Pour yourself a drink and I'll kill a few moments with that cryptic tale about the Princess and the Pea. It always made Cristian die. Laugh, should I say.

Once upon a time there was a worried Queen with a handsome son who needed a bride. The Queen invited a different Princess to stay at the palace each weekend and each weekend she performed the same ritual: after the maids had made up the bed in the guest chamber, the Queen went in and placed a pea under the mattress. At breakfast the following morning, she would ask the visiting Princess if she'd had a good night's rest. "Oh, yes, dear Queen, indeed I did," they would reply. And they were never invited back to the palace again.

This went on for a very long time. The Prince grew older, the Queen impatient. Then, a night came when the visiting Princess called servants to her chamber to complain that the bed was uncomfortable. The servants came running with another mattress, which they laid on top of the existing mattress and retired, blowing out the candles.

Twenty minutes later, the bell cord was pulled and the servants summoned once more. They brought a third mattress, a fourth, a fifth and sixth. Still the Princess was unable to sleep. Next morning, the Queen, acquainted with the night's proceedings, leaned across the table to ask the unerring question: "Did you have a pleasant night?"

"I am sorry, my good Queen, but I am afraid I did not. The bed was rather lumpy. I was unable to sleep a wink."

She turned away, shaking her head. Her long curls have the lustre peculiar to a black athlete's skin, eyes stolen from a lost kitten, a retroussé nose like a delicacy in a ribboned box, and those archer's-bow lips are drawn in the faintly pained, downward curve befitting a Princess.

The Queen clutched her hands across her abundant breasts and gasped. "Finally, there is someone with feeling, a Princess who is truly sensitive. You shall marry the Prince."

81

And so it came to pass. The church bells all across the land rang out to announce the royal wedding and the people smiled and smiled and everyone in the kingdom was happy.

"Why Daddy?"

Was my son a genius?

Why these unfortunates in their cretin cloaks of simple mindedness were overjoyed with an event extraneous to their own miserable lot is not germane to the tale although their happiness serves to dramatise the Prince's dilemma.

Sure, the Princess was a tasty dish to set before a future King but: one pea! She would have migraines. Allergies. Anal Retention. Say no when she means yes. Yes when she means no. Complain of premature ejaculation. It hurts. It's too big. It's so *small*. You're not doing it right. I've *never* had an orgasm. When he got angry she would call him a brute; his kindness would be ridiculed as weakness. Never lend friends money; or your car. People despise those who are good to them. The Prince would try to please her and the more he tried the more it would rasp against her many and divers sensitivities. Even Princes become jittery boys in the company of beautiful women. The princess, like the bogus virgin, knows how to be charming; when to be funny or witty; serious or sad; sincere, humble, pouting. They are manipulative. It is a gift like an ear for music. Men have it, too, maturing later, like French wine, a rare innate skill absent from my horoscope.

As the state architect, I have been loathed, venerated and occasionally bribed by enterprising girl graduates climbing the rungs of the Ministry, visiting my office wearing slit sided skirts and wriggling their thighs to ensure my view of their juicy attributes. And they are the ones who succeed, let me assure you. The still slim middle-aged matron heading a big company, the anchorwoman on the six o'clock news, the cabinet deputy: they were the young girls who knew how to put it about as they reached up at the same time to claw at the next notch on the slippery pole, not forgetting to kick their heels down into the faces of those left behind. Hey, fuck 'em.

I was the notch on the way, a swift hand job without a soupçon of respect. And without respect what are we? We are nothing. Less than nothing. We are an insect. A dead insect. The stain left by a dead insect. I am the state architect. *I want some respect*, the odd lay, a few friends who pop in from time to time, a message on the answerphone, a postcard, a bottle of wine. I'm not unique. I'm not special. Like you. Like most of us. Like all of us. I sit in my room staring at the walls wondering what it all means. I drink too much. Pee too often. Talk to myself. I have two parents, interred in the same urn and stored somewhere in the apartment here where they always felt out of place and remained out of place in the protean convolutions of Helena's decorating. I must have been adopted. I felt no connection to them. They were the landscape that quickly vanished as the craft of destiny set out across the sea of my life.

They were proud of me, I realise that. But they would have been just as proud without all the fuss; without the Palace.

I was held in the crushing grip of my own shortcomings, we all are: tenants locked in the prisons of mind and body and space and time; becoming tired and infirm; growing sores and lumps and new diseases; clambering like rats on a treadmill, breathing the thin venomous air from a sky arranged in lines above the rooftops. The inner man is so occupied being whatever it is he imagines he is expected to be, so absorbed conforming to traditions and conventions, only the freak has the courage to stand alone, outside the herd, and he either goes mad, goes to jail or goes into politics.

The rest of us are glove puppets, rising with a headache, working without interest, watching the clock peel away the rinds of the day until night falls on silent family homes where TV sets dispense their fare of violence, sex and soap: Will he marry her? Is she pregnant by another man. Or an alien? Or next door's dog? Is she really the daughter of the other woman. Has she got syphilis? Or AIDS?

And now the news: The Lion opens Environment Conference with a Giant Bonfire and we watch the flames as if hypnotised and we watch again thirty minutes later, junkies anxious for a fix. Re-read a newspaper article twice and the item will be remembered. A book leaves the residue of wisdom shared and a good book enjoyed will linger on the memory forever. Bad books should be abandoned after thirty pages and newsreels should be avoided. Television information does not remain in the mind. It is inertly received, effortless to swallow, like the white sugar slipped into everything. It is melted faux chocolate fed intravenously; cathode-coated leprosy furtively rotting the brain and persuading us to eat the same, dress the same, think the same, behave the same and, at the same time, believe we are oh so individual.

Television is the profoundest source of cerebral and social pollution since the invention of God. By constant repetition, all phenomena becomes actual, substantiated truth.

"I heard it on the six o'clock news."

We expect the newspapers to lie and read the lies daily in black and white. The TV broadcast is passing, chimerical, a sleight of hand, a trick of the eye, the eye watching us from the corner of every living room, bar counter, waiting room; watching like a tolerant adult with a retarded child capable of sitting motionless on a settee hour after hour being witlessly mesmerised and, worse, we pepper this tripe with commercials subtly louder, so jarring during our settee slumber we awaken as if from a soporific to paste jingles to our subconscious like the camp philosophy of greetings card quotes we stick on the refrigerator: *Happiness Is Never Saying No*; taking this viscous memoranda to the superstore where our fingers as if directed by a spell reach for the soap, soup, coffee from Colombia, crackers, cream cheese, the microwave Chicken Tikka Masala and, yes, it's so true, how can we be seen with a three year old motor; an antediluvian shaver; a clapped out lawn mower for the card table lawn; the fat wife needing health food, green food, polyunsaturates and will he marry her? Is she really a lesbian? Or a Venusian? On Uranus, the people make love by eating their partner's faeces. The romantic men of Neptune kill themselves after intercourse with large doses of bad poetry taken in rooms containing canvases of contemporary art. On Jupiter, underpopulated as it is, the male sex organ is situated in the index finger of the right hand, while that of the female is in the socket of the eye; sometimes left, sometimes right, depending on the time of the month and phases of the moons. On unseen Xerxes, where the denizens are self-effacing and sin predictable, reprobates are punished by being placed in a cage of mirrors.

"I heard it on the six o'clock news."

Royal prince in sex change sensation. Full, heartbreaking details. And coming up next there's a war in some ruin of a famine-racked nation where the debt is greater than the land value of its entire surface, the little black people with vacuous expressions blowing themselves to smithereens with weapons bought in the developed world and made to keep men in jobs, politicians in favour, women in magazines, the dog in whale meat, the First Minister in his Palace, Cristian in photographs folded in my wallet and we don't lift our voices and raise our fists because we are desensitised by television although, in polite homes, when guests appear, the volume control is gently caressed.

We are unconscious. We have submissively gone about our everyday trivia and survival while Armageddon stalks our every step. The predicament is universal, ubiquitous, so vast there appears to be no hope of changing anything, no point in trying. And where there appears to be no hope people grow passive, apathetic, withdrawn. There will always be a few exceptional individuals, the Evergreen fanatics who throw themselves under the wheels of limousines; in the path of oil tankers. But the great mass of people, encouraged by the tranquilliser in the corner of the living room, grow exhausted, acquiescent, as plant-like as the preposterous jade tree lurking amongst the debris on my desk. The lack of hope, the lack of individuality, deadens our will, our brain, even our movements.

God.

Eight

Allow me to wring out the last tear drop of wine. The moment appears to have come. I am not fatigued. I have no appetite or need for sleep. A decision is approaching, something elusive, like the faint breeze preceding rain. We Homo sapiens are losing the faculty for this function. We have computers to make decisions for us and, forced into making one alone, the process becomes as mysterious as the thirteenth sign of the Zodiac. A decision for me is the Siamese twin joined at the spine to depression; arising, loitering in the way of a drunk outside a closed bar, departing with mute reluctance. There is just me, here in this room; an empty bottle, Helena in Paris, Cristian under a blanket of earth. The Lion's insanity is complete and so are the ministry buildings that encircle the Palace. My fingers are twitching; my palms sticky, itchy. My job has been done.

I am free.

Or is there something else? A fag would help. Just a drag or two. For nostalgia's sake. There are brown spots on the backs of my hands, yellow marks in the crotch of my fingers. They smell of nicotine, exhaust fumes: Marten at the wheel of his car, the flames burning the back of my neck, the fire behind us planting a seed that would define the future, as a seed had been placed centrally on the last platform of the Great Pyramid prior to the capstone to send messages across the universe.

I open the bindings around the plans just as an author may open the pages of a book published long ago when he was a different person.

My work is pure genius. No, let me explain. It is a semantic point: the idea came from nowhere, snipped from the air without forebears or research. It was not a piece of artwork, an extension of the tangible, merely derivative, but something that transcends the normal cogitative process. It was drawn as a composer writes music to the metronome of Anton's seductions.

However outlandish it may seem to you, the worthy citizen who has been obliged to watch the Palace grow, it was during the times when the headboard next door was trying to break through the wall that my project became more defiant, more reckless, while remaining within the bounds of a pattern that began one memorable night when the moon's glow had fallen in a triangular beam across the paper clipped to my drawing board. Mildly stoned, my mind in a vacuum, I followed the expanding lines with a pencil, halted half-way and, using a set square, added two verticals. I joined them with a horizontal and thus completed a five-sided figure, a squat pentagon not dissimilar to a child's one-dimensional drawing of a house, something that only occurred to me much later.

Can you imagine my exhilaration? A path is made by laying one stone at a time. A new life commenced at that point, that night, the waste bucket filled with Kleenex, the full moon like a phantom ship on a sky storm-filled in stars. I tasted freedom and, yes, I know it reeks of hyperbole, but that's the only way I can describe it. I had found some hidden mechanism within myself. The artist was revealed. I had an idea growing inside of me and that idea had the rare quality of being both original and a touch ironic.

I was so excited. I'm excited still, by the memory, with the plans in front of me. The concept was basic, primitive, yet with precedents from antiquity: the columns of a portico developed from the trunks of trees driven into the ground to support the rafters of a herdsman's hut; the pagoda, a collection of decorative awnings, is merely the opium vistas of a Chinaman dreaming of standing one tent on top of another. I stared down at the sheet of cartridge and visualised four chambers that, when sketched in, had the appearance of pointed windows. I completed my vision with a set of double doors and, in the margin, wrote the word BRONZE.

I was exhausted but ebullient. I went down the passage to the bathroom like a sleepwalker passing Anton on his way back, a smile creasing his beard, his chest hairy and bare, a towel around his waist. His feet slapped the hall tiles.

"Unbelievable!"

"Good night."

"Certainly is, Tomas."

Bastard.

I washed my sticky palms. I slept like a baby and went through classes next day impatient to return to my drawing board. It wasn't until after supper that I was able to study my work and it was then, at that precise moment, that I made what was clearly to be the most important decision of my life.

It was the early days of spring in my fourth and final year at university, the time when Anton was creating the objects for his one-man show and Helena was expanding her repertoire. I had eight weeks in which to produce a finished architectural plan that would be marked by the tutors and determine my future. My contemporaries were busy drafting ideas for hotels, apartment blocks, environmentally friendly vacation homes with water wheels to generate electricity, functional structures with some fanciful mote of originality they believed they would one day build and, lamentably, none ever did.

My scheme was different. It was as grand as it was irresponsible and right from the beginning I gave it the grand name: The Palace of Democracy.

It grew. I studied my five flat surfaces and gave four of them a pentastyle colonnade, the five Doric columns supporting an arcade of Gothic arches. The arches in turn framed tall windows that would receive the sun in its passing glory before sending it on in such a way that, below the roof's five domes, the debating hall would always be criss-crossed in chiaroscuro bars of deepening and fading light, the effect like water running over rocks in an ever-changing motion that provides each pair of eyes with a distinct picture both consummate and transient; the union of Picasso's sand drawings and the neon installations being developed contemporaneously by various disciples of Duchamp.

Having adorned the building's side and rear walls in styles that migrated through time from mediaeval to the classical, the glass domes adding a further dimension to the cascading light, I reached the front wall in a mood that was distinctly rococo and not one of Biedermeier expressionism, as one critic noted in a Sunday magazine of alleged repute. Biedermeier, as architects learn, even if critics do not, was initially a mocking term for the philistine tastes of the German merchant classes and, while it has acquired with age a verdigris of respectability, it was not Biedermeier that touched my senses as a student, but the more decadent and haunting works of such diverse artists as Christo and Hieronymus Bosch.

In my mind I saw slabs of marble being hauled from Mount Pentili, where the stone for the Parthenon was quarried. But, having dispensed with any prudence during the design stage, I drew upon the practicable aspects of my education and was more pragmatic with the technicalities of construction.

I set about devising a system for manufacturing sections in pre-stressed concrete, these being strengthened by iron rods coated in titanium, to prevent corrosion, the sections slotting together before being veneered in a solution of polyurethane and marble dust. The carvings were moulded in fibreglass and, when sprayed in a resin formula blended with volcanic sand, they acquire the same time-polished quality as the granite revellers of Khajuraho. I sited a pair of Egyptian sphinxes as guardians beside the main entrance, the area above lit by a shield of armorial glass that, being a non-military man, appealed to the military tastes of the Lion. My original plan for the entrance doors called for the use of bronze but, there being so few craftsmen able to work traditional metals, the resin blends we finally employed turned out to be wholly satisfactory.

The overall effect, you must agree, is rather impressive: Greek columns supporting a baroque loggia, Gothic windows, Byzantine domes fringed by Norman crenellations, the heating pipes winding through the compound in a post-modernist style that mirrors the air vents in the cavity walls; Moorish spires adding a profound harmony over the tiers of laced mullions; a glorious pastiche that incited journalists to drop butcher's knives into their prose, describing my work as a masterpiece of architectural plagiarism; offal from a slaughtered madman; Female Circumcision; RAPE, screamed one headline and, the most famous of all:

This alliteration so appealed to contemporary tastes the word was seized upon by the tabloid press as a simile for all those tiresome and annoying things in life: the cheap and nasty, oil slicks, dog shit, chain stores, traffic, football managers, sleaze, politicians, prices; everything that is not quite how it should be and doesn't actually work when you get it home and take it out of the box.

As a chair has four legs, a broken chair is a pentangle; a one-eyed cat, rotting garbage, other people's children, the acid pong of the old, unemployment, unwanted pregnancy; everything foetid, cracked, snapped, splintered, shattered and nauseating; the obnoxious and odious; all that is plastic, artificial and vulgar was rolled flat and pressed into a pentangle. Chip a piece from a square of glass and what you have is a pentangle. "I got fired. The boss is a pentangle." The car's broken down; the wife's a slag; life's intolerable: it's a pentangle.

From all that is broken and sordid, it was only a short step for a pentangle to come to represent all that was corrupt and evil, resourceful diarists regaling us with their esoteric blah about the Inquisition, Nazis, the five pointed pentacle of necrophiliacs and Tarot card readers, assuring their own readers they had predicted the *pentangle-effect* an age ago.

Pith and Pulp Pushed into a Pentangle should have read, of course, Pith and Pulp Pushed into a Pentagon or, better, a Pentahedron. But, the slip having been made, there was never the will to put this wrong to right. Like fuck, pentangle has become a verb, adjective, noun, adverb and pronoun. Unlike fuck, it has found a home in the Heritage Dictionary.

By the end of the 1960s, the paper walls of social decorum and susceptibility had been ripped down. As I was growing up twenty years later, greed, dishonesty, hypocrisy, all that is coarse and second rate had become standard, accepted: the norm. We had exchanged our belief in the elusive eternal for faith in the external: in appearances, trivia, the designer label, the magazine promise. Win Free Sex. Get Good Head. SEND NOW. Money Back Guarantee. GO FOR IT.

"I've got a video of a sheepdog doing it with an eight year old."

"I'll come round with a couple of cans."

"He left his wife and six kids for a schoolgirl."

"Good on 'im. Must be getting my share."

"He nicked twenty grand from the bank."

"S'arright, he only did it for the money."

"Used to be a train robber…"

"Cunt."

"…before privatisation, of course."

They are acts that appeal to our innermost senses. We chuck the occasional priest and soap star to the wolves to mollify some dimly recollected tendency, to pacify the hanging threads of religious orthodoxy but, come on, let's be honest: we have in this new millennium finally rid ourselves of moral restraint and attained the veracity of our atavistic selves. We want to fuck our own thirteen old year daughter, strangle her mother, hack the neighbour to bits and take his mound of pelts to fill our cave. It is the reality of our genes. Incest is congenital; madness hereditary. We have come to believe only riches have importance and what is a stack of mammoth skins but money in the bank?

Into this environment of rape, everyday theft, murder, ball kicking philosophers, corrupt politicians, silicone breasts, AIDS and famine, my plans for a complex of new buildings had the power to shock the nation. I had created the *Catch 22* of the twenty-first century: I was an artist; controversial. I was despised.

Pith and Pulp Pushed into a Pentangle.

But there was a vital element these frothing castrators missed. It was an exercise; a polygamous marriage of styles to show that I understood the styles, just as a composer wields the same range of crotchets and quavers as his predecessors to shape a new piece of music, as Helena informed me, and I may well have mentioned.

"From the fascinating to the frivolous," wrote Ani Ivancheva, the critic, tottering into dotage and lusting after official patronage, a title, an honour, something to tell her she had once existed. It was my best review.

The criticism was easier to accept. It is the cross the artist must bear and, should he succeed, tricking the Gods, it will be borne on the backs of others. That being understood, the fact that I was to become an object of ridicule and, from the untiring Evergreens, the target of the most vindictive hate campaign in living memory, is something I continue to find insuperable. The campaign included poison pen letters to me and my family, and vile telephone calls that were so numerous and repugnant that for a time we had the apparatus removed from the apartment we had just moved into.

I would like to make one point very clear, a point these bellyaching censors chose to overlook: I designed the Palace of

Democracy, I did not commission its construction. I neither asked for nor expected to be elevated beyond my dreams or nightmares. I could not escape my fate, something the Greeks understood, as I could not escape my nature, as Marten and the Lion must have understood.

It is another of life's fey humours: for those who triumph, the Gods are ever eager for retribution. Whom the Gods wish to destroy they first make architects is a convenient if fatuous misconception. Whom the Gods wish to destroy they first make human, for all men are doomed. If man attempts to circumvent his destiny and shows signs of succeeding, the Gods kill his child.

The Palace was a fantasy. It was sketched at night to the sound of Anton Cesar's seductions and it all began, I would swear, the night of the full moon when he rolled Helena over and kissed her shoulder blades.

Helena was there from the start. My muse. My only love. Her words of encouragement, however frail, would be the substance that drove me on.

How could I have known I would receive the highest marks ever awarded in an architectural examination, a doctorate, a job with the government? I neither anticipated nor wanted the First Minister to leave the campus after his cultural inspection with my blueprints under his arm, hugged to his chest like a peace treaty, gripped as if in a steel vice by his long powerful fingers, his hand the hand of my fate, the hand that pointed through the years to this hushed room with its dull light, an empty bottle and a sudden sharp pain in my bladder.

Excuse me just for a moment.

A German baron of my acquaintance, when faced with the same pressure, has the civility to continue his discourse without taking leave for the amenities. I have watched the dark stain spread into a smile that brightens his eyes and warms into his lips. So many of life's small mysteries come clear at the moment of release. He rattles on like an old Swiss clock. Time rattles and grinds, sows and reaps. Only the past is eternal. The years accumulate. The lines deepen. Soon, I will be able to wedge credit cards in the corrugations of my brow. Time is amorphous, soft clay we fashion and fire into something instantly breakable.

I am tediously sober. Like my bladder, the wine isn't what it used to be. One of the bulbs in the bathroom has burnt out. The middle of the three mirrors above the basin is broken, smashed by Helena's bare fist one night when she just couldn't stand the music scribbled backwards on her brow a moment longer. The shards of glass showered the floor. She fell to her knees and searched among the pieces for a glimpse of the past, cutting her fingers so that she couldn't play her cello and I can't recall that I ever heard her play again. The wall tiles are from Spain, the colour of terracotta with ochre fleur-de-lis in each corner. The basin and bidet have brass fittings the maid used to polish to a shine that returned a misleading reflection.

I miss the maid. We never spoke. But, then, Helena and I didn't speak that much either. Everything was understood. I asked my wife only only once about Anton's avocations and she put a finger to my lips. When we left the art gallery the night of his vernissage she drew a line behind the past, in its dust, and I was happy.

We stopped somewhere for pizza. The food was a long time arriving and she leaned over to the next table. "May I?" she asked, taking a slice from the man's plate before he could say no. She returned the slice with interest when our pizzas came.

"Do you always do that?"

"I try not to do anything twice," she told me.

She ate with her fingers. They were long, strong fingers with hard pads on the tips of her left hand which she would use to tap out pieces of music she composed as she gazed at objects seen by no one but herself. She answered questions with shrugs, vague smiles, a long, strong finger that fastened my lips when I probed her secrets. We returned to my room. We stood over the drawing board in the moonlight and she blessed my plans with her interest.

"It's stupid stuff," I said.

"No it's not. It's what you do. And it's beautiful."

No one had ever said anything like that before and I spent years wondering what it meant. Her eyes were shining in the dark like fireflies, lighting her face with its complex of hinges and joints; it was a lovely face saved from prettiness by its intensity, its boyishness; a face with lost coves and hidden gorges, uncharted rivers, long stretches of sand dreaming of footprints; a face like a door glimpsed from the corner of the eye in a rush through an unknown city. I have drawn her face a thousand times and never found the key.

We made love and it was better than that time in the park. She took control, as she controlled her musical instrument, moving it between her long legs so that its sound box erupted in a deep and sonorous song. You have to be robust to play the cello. It's a cumbersome brute fond of knocking over house plants and precious porcelain. With Helena it was a dancer, supple, light as an illusion; yet frenzied in its climax, the boom of the bass notes encircling us in a wall of sound, a language without words. Music shows. It doesn't tell.

Helena made me feel as if I had been chosen for some special task, which is why when the First Minister took interest in my plans my surprise was genuine, but not total. It made sense that the Fates would be generous with me, in order to keep watch over her, a pure soul in a nasty world. She had left the Ursuline Convent for the conservatoire. She had a sister, Stella, her antithesis; a mother, Stella's clone; a dead father, a film star handsome man who rides a grey stallion through the photograph album with its black pages and captions in French chalk; standing on the foreshore with a child about his neck; on a flight of steps with two girls in matching sailor frocks, the roly-poly one smiling, the other seeing visions, her head to one side, eyes avoiding the camera lens.

She liked making love and playing the cello and combined these pursuits, vacating the bay windows when I returned from the office, leading me to the bed where her movements would continue a theme set by Elgar, Mozart, Mahler: spiny and victorious, slow and inspired, wistful, a trifle melancholic; sighing like a cat and feigning interest when I talked about the follies and misfortunes of my daily toil.

Helena never worked except for the occasional performance on the radio with a string quartet, an appearance at a café, or the concourse at the theatre where people ate prawn salad, sipping red wine as they waited for the play to begin. She could have been an accomplished soloist, they said, but was content to perform her solos alone in the bay windows and I have few recordings of her playing. "She lacks ambition," Anton said. "She lacks ambition," said her mother, said the other three parts of the string quartet. "You should push her, Tomas, what with your contacts," said Stella, circling the room on solid legs, on Sunday mornings before church, dropping ash over the sofa, on the lapel of my jacket. Helena would be staring from the window, the light from the balcony giving her the radiance of the Virgin in the old cathedral when the doors are flung open and an arrow of light sets fire to the darkness.

We were a beautiful couple, invited everywhere, desiring to go nowhere except back between the sheets where we played a duo for flute and strings. We would stand at cocktail parties gazing from the corners at each other, anxious to go home. We sat at dinner and while I listened to my companion on one side or the other, I was more interested in whatever Helena was saying or hearing across the table, her voice so soft people would lean closer and gather her words like tear drops from a stone Madonna. We would come home and make love and it was always good until that time when it wasn't. Cristian had been gone from us a long time and it seemed longer. I would hold her in my arms at night, stroking her long body as I had watched her each day stroking her cello.

Her breathing was even. I kissed her neck, her ear, her eye-lids. I cupped her small breasts in my hands and as I touched my lips to her nipple it lit a fuse inside her and she exploded, rolling on top of me, pinning me down, beating my chest, shoulders and face with her strong fists. She was screaming, not words, but a long, plaintive wail that cracked the plaster and made the windows rattle and woke the widows from their nightmares and stopped the late night drunks on their weary way home. I did not move. I felt no pain except the eternal pain. It was a relief. I was comforted by each blow. As she wailed, I wailed with her, two extinct animals crying for something never to return.

The beating came to an end and she collapsed into my arms sobbing.

"We have to pay," she said. "It doesn't come free."

The next day she was gone and her absence is as hard to bear as her suffering had been. We speak on the phone, not often, and say little.

I lift the phone now and listen to the hum so long a voice emerges from the void with advice that I replace the receiver. I do so.

Nine

Swish, swosh, shhhhh, ssssss, glurk, glurk, glurk.

In these words I wish to evoke the sound of water swishing and hissing over the porcelain, a gargle, a spit, a slosh and a slurp as the dregs run in a merry chase down the plug hole.

I am cleaning my teeth, ridding my mouth of the taste of whatever it is I haven't eaten, studying my face in the chip of mirror held by a sturdy screw as one may study a photograph of a group of friends taken twenty years before.

What hair they had; what bright expressions. The clothes are quaintly wrong and no one is quite as beautiful as we recall. We are unable to recount what was said, but we remember the texture of the air, the angle of the sun, the murmuring hum of insects like an evocation, a Lamaist chant that blots out the inanity of the everyday present and leads us back to the vespertine vaults of our ancestral spirit. We can hold in our mind's eye the colour of a butterfly's markings, the birdcall, the Chinese kite making erotic arabesques in the blue, blue sky and the words, the hopes, the broken dreams, all have gone, vanished like the dust blown from the top of a cherished book lost and found again. The past is the sound inside a music box, always profoundly sad.

I perceive on the frayed edges of my senses a withering vision of summer days when Cristian was learning to walk or to ride and Helena still smiled and there were friends to form a barricade between us and the barbed spikes of the critics. I probe the mysterious depths of the broken glass as if in the reflection a ghost will appear over my shoulder and I keep looking, hoping to recapture all that is gone. My search lacks vanity. Even incredulity. It is a critical examination, like Pandora with the sculpture she had made of herself.

If you spend ten minutes a day gaping at the looking-glass you get to strike off sixty hours from your life a year. Across the world there are countless clocks crunching through the crusts of time. Vanity is interminably consuming but so is chess. I once had a friend who was an expert on extinct South American Indian languages. Sofie is an art historian. With longer hair I could pass as Cronus devouring his son in Goya's painting. I am an atheist and an adherent to some god damn Almighty. When your child dies for no reason, *none*, you need some solace and what is there other than God? We need God to make sense out of the sheer, pointless insanity, which is life.

Life has no motive, no value, no future. We are as the ants: a collection of cells that explode, implode, then fade to nothing, not even memory. We need God because life is harsh and uncompromising and the harsher and more uncompromising it is, the greater the need. Why do more women attend church than men? They miss two periods, marry some boy at twenty and a month later, he's a bullying, drunken oaf. And why does he become those things? Because his life is meaningless and deep down in the poxed sewer of his subconscious he knows it's meaningless. Starving Africans; car crashes; dead infants with blue lips. I see no logic in living beyond our assignment. We have nature's obligation: to send on the seed. Then, it's just repetition.

William Burroughs said if you disregard the moral bullshit to which he didn't subscribe to anyway, selling heroin in the street was more acceptable than the iniquity of clocking on at a job. Lurking in

102

dark places with the aim of molesting schoolgirls on their way home for tea makes as much sense as a sideline as anything else. Better than stamp collecting. When a kingdom is conquered, the first duty of the invading army is rape. It's in the genes. Kill the men, then get down to the business of rape. It's only since we repressed this impulse that Man has felt obliged to level his spleen on the planet. I blame the feminists. The old ways had a certain *je ne sais quoi*: ten years of battle with a broadsword, the occasional thirteen year old to violate, then a nasty death at thirty. Is it any worse than university, a mortgage, uncontrollable kids and corporate disappointment; facelifts, pensions, the long lonely wait for the guillotine door of the crematoria? I scrutinise my cannibal face to find some reason why I was born and must conclude, as did Cronus, I'm sure, that it is better to be dead than alive and better never to have been born at all.

What mulish strain in humanity makes us get out of bed each morning and bear that undetermined chin into another new day; running for the bus with the daily paper (trying in vain not to let your tongue slip out of your gob as you gawk at the tits), flipping to the TV pages for the nightly narcotic? Friends never call. The telephone never rings. When did you last sit back with a belly laugh? All life is monstrous: the widows with the air of understudies for a play never staged; *M* Erich, liftman for a broken lift; Helena with her dead child and the work of dead composers at her fingertips; the elderly man who grazed some stray nerve ending the other night when loneliness and hunger marched me off through the crumbling ghetto of the Old Quarter.

"Look at that fucker. The fucking bastards."

He bent to retrieve a cigarette only half smoked which he straightened and concealed. I was following, listening to the commentary, a wholly rational review of a thanatoid society thriving on poverty and waste.

"Fucking bastards. You're all bastards. Fuckers. Fucking fuckers. There's another fucker. Fucking bastards." He bent again.

It was a damp night, warm and close. My shirt was sticking to my back. The shops were in darkness except for the liquor store run by a grim Armenian eating black olives from a tin. He gave me a dubious look, as if my request for a packet of cigarettes were a code, glancing at me over his shoulder, glancing at the door. He handed me the change and his expression brightened, his lips parting to reveal an acropolis of broken teeth.

"Is hot," he said.

"Yes."

"Is hot."

"Yes."

By the time I caught up with the tramp, he had reached a small square lit by the cheerless lights of a bar. Some people talking loudly were on their way out and another party was waiting for them to pass before they entered. The old man was muttering obscenities at another dog end. I slipped the packet of cigarettes into his hand and his reaction fused the two groups of strangers into a hostile crowd.

"You fucker. Filthy fucker. Fucking filthy fucker. You, you fucking fucker."

His yellow eyes leaked streams of tears as he tore the cellophane from the packet. He removed the cigarettes in clawing handfuls, ripping them to shreds and casting the pieces about him.

"Poor man," I heard a woman behind me say. "It's so sad," her companion replied in the upper-lower-middle class accent of the million left behind. "Pillock," said one of the men as I turned into a ring of carnival masks all glaring at me with unimaginable hatred.

"Fucking fuckers," the tramp was saying.

I hurried on.

The streets grew steep and dormant. The cobbles shone like black puddles. Bloated pigeons too fat to fly compelled me on a crooked course that led to a bar crouching between two derelicts, the sign above the door promising beer made from spring water. I slid inside with the shifty demeanour of a rat escaping into a drainpipe and emerged on the deck of a ship in a bottle, a foundered vessel run aground in the past. A man was strumming a Country and Western song on a twelve-string guitar accompanied by an accordion player with a bald head and a skirt of white hair that fell like a wig to the tartan squares of his cowboy shirt.

The landlord was polishing a glass. His movements froze and he eyed me suspiciously.

"Bitter," I said.

"Straight glass?"

I nodded along with the music.

> *Freight train, freight train, going so fast*
> *Freight train, freight train, going so fast*
> *Please don't tell them what train I'm on*
> *So they won't know where I've gone...*

The guitarist wore a cage around his face and in its bars perched a harmonica. The accordion player threw his head back to sing and in the excitement two women hurled themselves into a frenzied dance. The men watched hungrily. There were about six of us, not counting the midget, whom I didn't notice until later, a pack of werewolves crossing the steppes of their forties, a wilderness not quite one thing nor the other: the old age of youth; springtime of old age? They had lots of hair about their faces, dead eyes, tattoos like fungus crawling from collars and sleeves, marking hands with swallows, fingers with riddles. The women moved like clockwork drummers just rewound, one plump from morning biscuits, the other thin as a lizard, a snake spiralling up her thigh and disappearing under her leather skirt.

The homunculus - he was wearing ballet slippers and black tights - had commenced an elaborate jig. The rest of the men, moored like fishing boats to the bar top, clapped and whistled, urging him on, beating time with their boots, the movement slurping beer from their glasses like intermittent rain. The skinny woman had removed her shoes and was slithering over the sodden floor in her stockinged feet.

> *When I die won't you bury me please*
> *Way down yonder on Chestnut Street*

"Don't make music like that no more."
"Nah.!
"Love it."

> *So I can hear ol' Number Nine*
> *As she comes rolling down the line*

The barman must have noticed the tear in my eye. "Another drink, Guv?"

There was a smile straining the corners of his mouth, about his face that self-congratulatory look of recognition I'd seen so often in others. I was wondering with customary uncertainty if I should explain myself, lie, or apologise for something for which I did not feel apologetic. According to Oscar Wilde, whatever realised is right. The supreme vice is shallowness.

"Yes, yes I will," I said.

"S'arright. Anything else I can get you?""

"No."

I went to pay.

"S'arright, Guv, on the house this one."

We were communicating. We are herd creatures. They put Nijinsky in jail for giving his money away to the poor: the eternal nemesis. You see a beggar with his hand out and the herd man has the ready and accepted response: malingerer, wife beater, foreigner, bogus asylum seeker coming over here to get our dole and take our jobs and fuck our girlfriends. And why don't they work? I'll tell you why they don't work: they don't work because they don't want to work. That's why they don't work. They hang about the station with faces like yesterday's leftovers, then drive home to subsidised flats in a Volvo. Parasites. Breeding like rabbits. Disgusting. Someone ought to do something. Inject the lot of 'em. Castrate the bastards. Send 'em back where they come from. Charity begins at home. Pass the bucket.

Another pig's trotter?

There's little I dislike more than people sitting around a groaning dinner table with ample bellies talking about beggars with bank accounts, gypsies with safety pins, house maids hard to train, moronic nannies, impolite airline personnel and shop assistants nose-picking and cretinous. You know who they are.

Sure, I know it's a mistake. I toss the odd coin in the pauper's styrofoam cup. I help others in this haphazard and helpless way. Not because I believe it will do any good; not as balsam for a bad conscience. It is merely a habit that makes me consider that alarming cliché: Give a man a fish and you feed him for a day; give him a fishing rod and you feed him for life. As long as there is an endless supply of fish. And there is not. We have killed the rivers, maimed the oceans, raped the fish. Life is sordid. The human race is doomed because we lack the imagination to open our eyes and see what it is we are doing to the planet and what the planet means to ourselves.

Instead of waiting with famished forbearance like our good fathers, we want those fresh little vegetables so admired by Truman Capote all through the year and to capture this bounty the hydroponic corporations have gobbled up the land and are devouring the subterranean lakes formed in the Ice Age, the process dehydrating, calcifying and mummifying Mother Earth. We cannot stop. It is the will of the herd. You fear the herd. Despise the herd. You yearn to be a part of the herd and, when you find you're outside, forever outside, you sit down with a bottle of wine and a cry that rises up from your bowels and moves through the intestines, a great, wailing lament, not for the world, not against the police agents who would have you locked up if they could read your thoughts. No, you are sending up smoke signals to all those other lost souls who sit up late at night with a bottle of wine, a typewriter, a note pad, a blinking blue computer screen beside an open window. There are other elephants gone astray, ostracised by the herd, and together, we form our own herd, an internet of drunks and cross dressers, artists in garrets, the sons of Kafka, toiling in a bank by day, scribbling at night; the midget doing his thing, the snake woman propelling herself from side to side in such a way that I felt as if I were watching a marionette from the vantage point of the puppeteer and, from this perspective, she inspired in me a sorrow so profound I felt pity for her, her children who steal cars, the policemen who chase them, their father who has vanished, Helena in Paris and Cristian, a tiny pile of phosphorescent bones gleaming under the earth. I felt sorry for myself and for mankind, for all the dead fishes in the dead oceans, and all the self-styled geniuses who work in solitary confinement searching for signals that never come and they won't come because they're not being sent. The woman and her stumpy friend were dancing together but they remained alone as we are all alone: everything that lives, decays and disappears like the billion pinheads of sperm that die on the altars of fornication for every seed that connects, a seed invisible to the naked eye that, nonetheless, conveys with it a soul, memory, history, past lives and an inclination to join the herd.

"Another?"

Like a bidder at auction I used my chin in affirmation and watched the brown stuff swirl into the glass, the reverse of water going down a drain. It foamed over the rim and I had to adjust my stance to the tilt of the universe to get it down. I had turned away. The music had paused. The men were tossing out opinions like life lines from a listing tanker, quaffing drinks with desert thirst, hammering

109

glasses on the bar. I heard the names of football teams, politicians, actresses. Somebody was trying to sell somebody else a motorcycle that had belonged to a retired organist who had used it only once a week to take his wife to play bowls.

"Hey, it's you. The architect."

The thin woman was standing at my side with a look of sheer wonder in her kohl-farded eyes. She appeared familiar and my heart sank like a mine shaft when I realised who it was.

"Baby," I said.

"No one calls me that now. It's Barbra." She shrugged, as if in appreciation of the impermanence of all things.

I bought her a drink.

"Bleedin' hell, fancy meeting the architect."

I bought her another drink.

"Just goes to show, dunnit. Fought you'd've been gawn."

We became cheerful. Then happy, as cancer patients in New Zealand are happy with their plug of Manali. She told me the joke about two whores discussing a customer who always came in wearing a crown of thorns. "Dunno who he is, but he fucks like a gawd."

I laughed. I remembered the joke and I remembered this incredible skill: I opened my mouth and out it came: *laughter*.

It's amazing what three pints can do.

Barbra was starting to look less like a hag. I could even spot the remnants of Baby in the crevices below the make-up, as one sees the mystery of the pretty girl in the wedding photo thirty years on.

The duo embarked on another piece; the midget was standing on the bar measuring his height against a column of coins.

Barbra's shoulders were rising and falling. "Shall we go?" she said.

We moseyed off through the pigeon shit and litter and I had a feeling of déjà vu, the grim streets, somnolent and empty, burnt out cars, wild dogs. Even the graffiti had graffiti. We climbed three flights of concrete stairs to an apartment where her two sons who would grow up to steal cars were sleeping the sodium pentothal sleep of infants.

"I don't like to leave 'em but it would take a war to wake these two."

We were standing in the doorway of a windowless room where the set of bunk beds and a chest of drawers occupied the entire space. A step across the hall led to the living-room, waist-deep in assault rifles and spacecraft, the piles of laundry filling two armchairs having the look of a pensioner couple in a suicide pact. The bookshelves, void of books, held a menagerie of china dogs and coy girls with wind-whipped skirts showing china knickers.

An ancient Alsatian was asleep on the couch. Barbra stroked his head and his eyes blinked open. "Come on, Rex, make room for someone else."

The dog stretched, came to its feet and farted. "Thank you very much," she said, turning to me with a smile. "He always does that."

On a television the size of a child's coffin, glued in sticky rings, were some glasses and a bottle containing four fingers of cognac. Barbra poured two measures and, as she talked about Nico, her husband, a curious energy entered her features. He was so good looking. All the girls fancied him. He had wanted to open a bar or a pool hall or a night club or a discotheque or a roller-blading rink or a long haul trucking business but his partners always let him down. He

111

did six months for nicking some porno videos but he didn't let that stop him. Now he's in security. It's hard to imagine Nico in uniform. Works nights. Guards a store. Loves wearing a gun, he does. He knocks me about a bit but not so as it matters. Nico says women like being knocked about. They're all slags and he knows what he's talking about. I mean, can you imagine having the same bloke every day? I like Nico enough, he's so handsome, but variety's the spice as I always say.

She took off her damp shirt to show me the bruises and I remembered Baby's breasts, two lively chipmunks that had withered into goatskin bags. She unzipped the leather skirt, removing it with the grim etiquette of a dignitary unveiling a plaque. I had forgotten about the snake. She turned in a slow circle so I could see the tattoo in all its splendour. The slippery green skin of the creature circled her thigh, glided over the extruded bones of her hip, crossed her stomach and buried its head in her crotch.

"It was a present from Nico," she said and looked like one of the china girls showing her knickers on the bookshelves.

We started kissing for something to do. Her tongue had the taste of uncooked squid. We fucked on the couch, in the matted basket of dog's hairs, and it was like fucking a hole in the ground. Ten years before Baby had filled my mind when I had spent the night with Pandora. Now, it was Pandora who came into my thoughts. Where had Baby gone? Whatever happened to Pandora?

"Didn't-cha know?" She lowered her voice: "She became a man."

Barbra closed her eyes and her face contracted with a couple of fake spurts, which was kind. She rolled over and told me she knew what I liked. I buggered her thinking of Anton Cesar and came with a painful gush like a boil being lanced.

We finished the bottle of cognac. She checked on the boys. Sound asleep. Out like lights. Little devils. They look just like their dad. He's a real bastard. S'funny thing, handsome blokes are always bastards. A couple of his business contacts were here the other night, while he was at work. I'll never know if Nico set me up. I was on top of this big lump named Toni and in waltzes his mate, drops it out of his pants and climbs on board. Well, you could have waited, I told him. I felt just like a side of beef in a butcher's, turning me one way, then turning me over and doing it the other. I acted as if I liked it and I did a bit. I mean, it was the first time and you know what I always say: variety's the spice. I'm going to bring my brother next time this Toni says, you've got room for a third, and he pokes his fat finger in my mouth. What a pentangle. They were gentlemen, though. They left me a bit of change.

As she fell silent the dog returned. He sniffed the couch prior to jumping back on, farted and fell asleep. Barbra waved away the smell.

"He always does that."

Ten

It was one-thirty. The night was warm. I heard a child scream. There was a loud clatter behind closed windows, a thump, then a prolonged whimper that faded as I made my way down the hill towards the bridge.

I was dying for a cigarette and searched the gutter for a dog end. "You fucking, fucker," the tramp had called me and yet, I had detected no malice in his words and, in his eyes, merely a serene distaste, not for me, the individual, but the whole of humanity. It was a look that, for some reason, suggested the mute acquiescence I have seen on the faces of middle-aged black women, an expression which comes from a lifetime of being exploited by fathers and brothers, husbands and sons, employers, racists, football fans. These women have no arrogance, expectations, ego. They are, as no bishop ever will be, in a state of grace. They embrace their suffering and through it find deliverance. Friedrich Engels said freedom is the recognition of necessity and I've never quite known what he meant.

I walked along the embankment above the sunken highway, the smell of sulphur in my nostrils, my thoughts pounding like the throb of a hangover.

Twenty years had gone by since the First Minister had marched off with my blueprints and, from that day, everything moved so fast I have been chasing time ever since, running to remain motionless, events and incidents layered one on top of another, sealing my fate as if inside a biscuit tin childishly buried for future generations to find. While Anton was exploring the dark mysteries of Helena, I was sitting in the moonlight, pencil in hand, a plan taking shape. When I was making love to Helena after she'd been discarded for Sofie, my creation was growing, constantly growing, and it was while we were still waiting for our results that I was told to attend a meeting at the First Minister's office.

The summons came through the university. My tutor mentioned it casually, after class. "And smarten yourself up," he said. The semester was coming to an end. Our projects were complete. There were a few especially talented students whose work had consistently been inventive and, when we learned that I, Tomas Sala, with plans considered mere foible, had achieved what can only be described as miraculous results, we were too inexperienced to realise that in every pie we would find a fingernail.

My appointment with FM was on a Thursday morning. It was the end of May and I stood alone in his office staring out from the windows, nervous sweat ringing my shirt, my neck constricted by a tie borrowed from Anton: the symbol of someone on their way, he had said: red for confidence, gold for success, blue for the bourgeoisie. He understood the colour scheme of things.

The trees in the park were swaying. I could see the zoo, a jungle in miniature at the centre of the lake, the fountain throwing out crystal bouquets. Swallows chiselled arabesques from the sky and the river, meandering through willows with silver leaves, was sluggishly making its way out to sea. The Lion's secretary, tall as a tower, thin as a duchess, had closed the door behind me. The Great Mason was on his way.

Clouds were circling the distant hills. I loved the city at that time of year, in the days when the seasons were clearly defined. Winter coats with pockets full of mothballs had been put away in the back of wardrobes. The park was a beehive of toddlers, mothers, old people pleased to be seeing another summer, young lovers glued at hip and arm, the future before them.

I was planning to visit Egypt in July and intended asking Helena to join me. She came from the conservatoire each day with pieces of music she would hum as she drummed the drawing board, pushing her hair from her face, a labour of mythical repetitions. We made love, the light turning orange, Helena lying back with obscure comments about her life, her hopes, the words on her lips taking on special significance. Her eyes were flakes of sky dropped by the swallows and in them I saw my dreams as I spoke in the same fragmentary way about my own world. We were private people reluctant to reveal ourselves. She knew by instinct I wouldn't bother her, change her, redraw her. I strummed the harp strings of her rib cage, an aviary for lost kites and melancholic angels, the near motionless hand on my spine like a hand on a rudder guiding the paper boat of my childhood to the centre of a lake where it sank with its cargo of maternal silences and nightmares filled with mirrors and fire. The perfume of those long afternoons, the sweet and faintly acrid tang of yesterday's flowers, made a canopy over the narrow bed, a shelter to guard me from memories of smoke and uncertainty. Helena had no strong views, political allegiance, no desire to judge others or be judged. We made love, our bodies entwined like the swirling letters of a monogram, clinging to each other until a dead arm or cramped leg compelled us to part. A glass of wine. A cigarette. I would glance at my drawings in the encroaching twilight, Helena like a pasha wrapped in a sheet turning the pages of architectural books, locating themes I incorporated in the Palace.

"What about a dome?"

"What about five of them?"

"Yes," she says and leaps from the bed like a mermaid.

Books quickly bored her. I would sit at the drawing board armed with a pencil, the picture of a dome, and she would play her music, refuelling the small room with gypsy reels and invented rhythms.

We have this fantasy: a vision of sprawling out in the sun like a caterpillar on a leaf, legs crossed at the ankles, hands behind your head, the clouds in bullfights across the *sol y sombra* of the open sky; a book, perhaps - Rimbaud? António Lobo Antunes? Orwell? Martin Amis? Márquez? - a free day on the riverbank, the sound of bubbling water, a bottle of wine with a friend, conversation worthy of being remembered. Nothing lavish.

There was once a king in ancient Greece who said on his death bed that there had been three things in life he had wanted and never had: a house by the sea, a canary in a cage and some basil in a pot.

Dreams are often so small they are easily misplaced. People quote Rimbaud at those irksome dinner parties without reading his poems.

Where was I?

In the Lion's den.

The damp rings in my shirt had spread into lakes by the time FM appeared and I gazed with Downs Syndrome eyes across the empty space between us, my mouth dropping involuntarily.

Seeing the great man face to face came as a shock. He was not as tall as I had always thought, although I had seen him many times, on television; even at the university. He was shorter than me, of course, but gave the impression of bulk, of power, of a missile that had been wound up and was ready to fire. He filled the room, moving quickly on stunted legs, raising his left arm to take me in a nonchalant embrace, as one embraces a statue for a photograph, then moving on, both arms windmilling the air as he spoke about things unknown and inexplicable to me.

He stopped and pointed out the window. "We are surrounded by fools," he roared, storming off again, clenching his fist and hammering it on the surface of a desk berthed with asinine precision below a portrait of himself.

The office was furnished in pieces of heavy oak and tubular steel, each placed geometrically as if without the impediment of human influence. I studied him from different angles during the ten minutes of his peregrinations and underwent a confused mixture of awe, fear and stupefaction. I felt as if I had been punched in the solar plexus, plunged into hot oil. My skin peeled away and I was born again, an apprentice in the abstruse domain of the black arts. I was in the company of a magician; an omnipotent being, not one of saintly mien, like a communist priest, but in the murky aura occupied by hanging judges and ritual butchers.

He poured two measures of whisky, added ice and passed me a glass, assuming that I drank in the middle of the morning, as a man who plays golf assumes God in His Heaven enjoys a four handicap.

He had squirrel red hair that was exceptionally lush and, sweeping back in one curling wave, it had earned him the sobriquet

118

'The Lion,' an unfortunate choice for one whose jungle would one day be a five-walled compound where unicorns roamed in search of fairy tales, and plastic gargoyles screamed at the wind. It is generally acknowledged that women with red hair have rebellious carnal desires and, once stimulated, exude the ripe stench of the stable. The Lion had that odour about him at all times and, though lacking when measured perpendicular to the ground, his big hands, feet and Pinocchio nose were visual evidence of the fable that he was hung like a dinosaur, words I have heard whispered with adoration, never irreverence.

His features were generous tending to the grotesque: a firm round chin like a dinner plate piled high with Negroid lips and a nose like the beak of a flightless bird. He had deep set, hypnotic blue eyes embellished with thickets of red hair in parasols over each lid and in a thatched roof that met across the bridge of that splendid proboscis. This visage appeared to have been hacked from a block of stone shot through with vermilion ore and sat like a sculpture in progress upon the plinth of his muscular body. The whole created the impact of a dense and reckless energy, the force of a sociopath safely impervious to all reason and all opinions but those assembled to suit his passing edification.

He was wearing the tie of the Reform League over a white shirt and an impeccable dark suit. Across his vest, hanging in loops, was a gold chain, the pocket watch he rarely summoned to his palm beating out the rhythm of the ages, this obsolete custom a link to the past, the closing century, and all those centuries beyond number when monarchs spun legends from their audacious and virile feats. The Lion, and that gold watch and chain were for me its symbol, was renowned for his mediaeval passions. He ate, drank, roared like a

119

beast in rut and required women as a growing boy requires cooked meals, at least one, or preferably two or three new conquests a day, essential to quieten the torments of his tyrannical seed and still the mace of his ministerial being. His capacity, coupled with his reputation for taking only beautiful women to his bed, made every woman curious for his touch and husbands, too, hoping for a leg up the professional ladder, could be seen at public functions presenting their spouses to him with the air of fishmongers with the season's fresh haddock.

He was barely forty, younger than me now, and had seized power for the Reform League after wandering in the political wilderness for more than a decade. While the conventional parties had been grinding themselves into the ashes of their petty and irrelevant squabbles, the Lion and his followers had been chipping away at the nation's heart with ominous reminders of our loss of sovereignty, our borders being pierced by alien hordes, the mosques and temples standing where our churches had stood, the weird and wondrous vegetables appearing in the market place where our good apples had once been heaped in brisk and shiny piles. The League marched with brass bands playing, flags waving, the hymns they sang reminding the good citizens that when Jesus left his father's workshop in search of knowledge, it was to our green and pleasant land where he had come.

The Lion rejoiced with irate passion the victories of old, all those centuries of incessant slaughter, which have made us what we are, and of which we remain so proud. We had shed seas of blood and, as we listened to his reminiscences we, too, saw a vision, his vision, and it revealed, not the horror, but the image of all our ambiguous desires. We heard the angelus peal. We were reborn from the dregs of our brain dead and dreary selves. We saw a new world like the old world freed from the computer, the scientist, the thinker and administered by the patriot, the primitive: a world ruled by grandeur and magic. Arrogance is the privilege of the young and in the Lion there was hope, a fresh face, new and full of vigour.

The collapse of communism during my student years had sent out shock waves that ruptured the foundations of our decaying society. What had been seen as a monumental achievement was soon recognised as a time of uncertainty, of transformation. The factions of East and West were a pair of withering protagonists from a jaded soap opera, the demise of one a forewarning of the decline of the other. We were at the end of an era. Between the end and the beginning a moment of contemplation is required. Between the problem and the promise of a solution stood the Lion.

Socialists and conservatives had moved to the centre ground occupied by liberals, with policies that were interchangeable and aspirations of achieving the solitary goal of acquiring and maintaining power. Politicians must appear to follow the demands of the people: democracy's grand illusion. Pledges are made because the opinion polls tell our elected leaders and prospective usurpers they will be popular making those pledges. The traditional parties had clearly lost their grasp on this basic premise. We were ready for change. The Evergreen Alliance promised to save the world. The Lion promised the world.

The election, the one we all remember, was close and, when the Lion led the Reform League to victory, we anticipated the League and the Evergreens pursuing the customary diversion of moving in and out of power every five or ten years, switching from government to opposition and back again like the motions of the moon. But the Lion was more canny and persuasive than his enemies had given him credit for. He had taken power from a government too bloated and corrupt to hang on any longer. He drove the brainiest and the best into exile, cut welfare, put stooges with tit fetishes in the editor's chairs in newspapers, closed the hospitals, emptied the mental homes and made everyone as mad as himself.

Our new leader perceived innately and was masterful at exploiting the essential principle that society's wheels are greased by the force of hatred: the upper classes hate the middle class from where they have escaped; the middle class hate the working class for the same reason, resenting the upper class for the downward sneer of their hatred; the workers hate everyone: the rich with their chirpy accents; the toadying bourgeoisie with their vulgar wives; the people from the north despise those from the south and those from the east despise the west in a criss-crossing configuration; they hate neighbours, foreigners, rival soccer teams, the criminal classes, whom they fear, and the underclass haunting the edges of their communities like birds of prey waiting to swoop and drag them down below decks on the Marie Celeste.

The Lion was able to cull support from every part of the structure except the very bottom and, with a series of astute ploys with the polling system, they lost their vote and no longer mattered. A more revolutionary manoeuvre occurred at the end of his first term in office: those people who failed to exercise their franchise were presumed to be content with the prevailing administration and their non-vote was attached to the government's tally. The bill was rushed through the

House but, for all its knocks, it arrived in one piece on the statute books.

The changes were subtle at first. They became less subtle. They became outrageous. And they continued in a way that the Lion has so altered our political process, our culture, our very thinking; he has become so enamoured of his own power, I cannot imagine him relinquishing it except with the aid of a knife between the shoulder blades. More than the Bolsheviks, the peasants who stormed the Bastille, or the bewigged sages who drafted the American Constitution, he has transformed the shape of society from the traditional pyramid: lower, middle and upper classes in diminishing blocks, into a sphere, a slippery globe where, through the fostering of phobias and confusion, each group is so desperate to hang on to what they have, they would rather see the Lion at the helm than some Evergreen lunatic who wants to save the planet.

Piss on the planet. We are frightened people. Frightened for our property, our daughters, our lives. We are afraid of inflation, taxation, the stock market dipping, the Chinese expanding, the Americans imploding. We are afraid of hospital charges, unemployment, phone bills and extraterrestrials. We need strong leadership. We need the Reform League, so marvellously named for there has never been a "league," but for the smattering of grubby-kneed sycophants who bathed in the reflected glow of their champion and, then, the Lion who leads them has no wish to "reform" society, except to take it back into the dark age of some indifferent monarchy such as the type he swiftly eased aside, dusting off the king for ceremonial occasions when he stalks the shadows wearing the expression of a man who has returned from the embrace of his lover to the wife he can no longer bear. The

123

monarchy had made the fatal error of misbehaving while *not paying taxes*. It had taken an age of interminable proportions for the good citizens to awaken to this grotesque anomaly, but the Lion had the courage and wisdom to put this wrong to right.

He curled the ends of his moustache, downed a swig of scotch, took me once more under his arm and, as we stared out from the window, I wondered how he had achieved the optical illusion, this freak of stature: the First Minister was short, not a circus dwarf, but not far off. He was a man who counted in quarter centimetres, as Napoleon might, Simon Bolivar, Franco, or Hitler, FM's inspiration, I assumed, for standing the king and his ministers two steps below himself when they posed for the cameras.

We moved from the window to the desk. He opened a drawer and pulled out my plans, leafing through, stabbing various pages with a finger, pointing that same finger into the trees. He dashed back to the window and back again to the desk, taking me with him like a long, vacillating shadow. A bubble of saliva had worked its way to the corner of his mouth and was threatening to roll down his chin.

"Let's kick arse," he said - he was partial to war films - jerking the spit globule with his tongue, washing it away with the last swallow of his drink, staring at me in such a way that, had I been born a woman, I would have ripped off my clothes right there in the office and screamed fuck me, fuck me, fuck me. Indeed, now, twenty years later, that's just what he has done, me, and everyone, the whole murmuring, curdled class of the *not-quite-discontented*, those who vote according to their fears and material interests and, these days, of course, express their approval by not voting at all.

124

Am I slow?

Helena said so, kindly, as a statement of fact: Sofie is rich; Anton is fat; Tomas is slow.

"Wake up. Wake up. You're living in a dream."

Darling, it was where I wanted to live. I hated the past. The present, that present long ago, was a fantasy, the Palace of Democracy the invisible structure that held the illusion in place.

My plans had been taken away, I imagined with other plans, but I had no notion of why. Can you imagine how the ghost of Van Gogh felt standing at the back of the auction room watching his Sunflowers being knocked down for millions? Little in life makes much sense and much makes no sense at all. I had no idea what the great man was talking about and listened as one listens to the ravings of a drunk out of politeness and alarm.

He was going on about shapes. "Five's always been my lucky number," he exclaimed, adding the merry non sequitur: "We're going to do it if it's the last thing I do." We trailed back to the window.

"Perfect," he said, punching the air, then spreading his arms like a father showing his heir all that one day would be his.

We stood there, looking out at the trees beyond the river. We were on the top floor of the former administrative offices, later pulled down, with a view across the city to the far hills, a shrinking band of undulating meadows around a throbbing cauldron of interlacing roads, factories, apartment blocks, an elaborate cat's cradle of telephone wires and power cables. The fingers of tall chimneys poked over the horizon with streamers of smoke in brown, yellow, and black.

"Bootiful!"

125

Our near vision was grey, endless buildings with endless lives going on inside them, the concrete plane broken solely by the green oasis of the park.

Beyond the river I was obliged to surface for the sunken highway, ran Victory Avenue, lined with the statues of heroes often quoted by the Lion. The parallel avenues running north from Victory Bridge and the Bridge of the Martyrs, begin their inward curve at the same point and intersect at the site's northern peak, ergo: the park sat within the boundaries of a pentagon, the very shape the moon and I had chosen for my final project at university.

All life is absurd.

"Perfect," the Lion said again.

He had his hand on my arm and as he applied pressure it felt as if I were in the grip of an electric door on a metro train about to leave the station. He began talking about Versailles and the Great Wall of China. "We will build something future generations will look back on and they will say we were men who believed in freedom."

Under the tenure of the old parties, whole neighbourhoods had perished to make way for new roads. New roads attracted more cars that kept men in jobs, supplying a need for more new roads in the inevitable cycle of creation and destruction that found the First Minister with the sudden desire to be known for what he had put up, not pulled down. As the past is always with us in the petrified history of architecture, it was the future calling and it was there where the Lion wanted to leave his footprints.

"I noticed immediately," he said, turning to look at me for the first time, studying me with the puzzled frown of someone who has acquired a piece of bric-à-brac at a flea market and can't imagine why.

126

We shook hands and I was shuffled out into the corridor. "Don't go too far. I'll push this through in a month," he shouted and I stopped. He was standing in the open doorway, his big hands on his hips, his face excited, as red as his hair.

"I'm going to build the Palace of Democracy," he roared and shut the door.

Eleven

These thoughts came back to me that night in the old city. A few more people had taken to the streets, gliding by coughing, gasping for air like feeding fish. It was like walking under water in a darkened aquarium. I remembered the smell of those streets when I had been a student and it had changed: the fusion of dirt and piss surrendering to the overpowering corruption of sulfur, yellowing the sky by day and obscuring the sky at night. There were no stars, no moon. A few meagre lamps hovered in the gloam and left blotches of light like stains on the grey stone buildings. I could hear rats snuffling about in the piles of waste.

I went home and opened a bottle of wine and I am doing just that at this moment.

Glug, glug, glug.

It's a wonderful sound, the first laps of wine gurgling into the glass, swirling in serpentine loops, growing still like a resplendent jewel, cold and deeply mysterious.

There is a psychological formula that echoes through the opening of every bottle of wine. You tell yourself you are only going to have one glass but, as soon as you have taken the first sip, you refill the glass; thus, one glass is one glass plus a sip. The neck is void but the body of the bottle remains full. You have a second glass, sighing as you go through the extra sip routine, only now the sip is a good swallow, a slug, a half glass. It is at this point that you remove the cork from the corkscrew, pinch off the mangled threads, and push it decisively back into the bottle.

The bottle is half full; note the optimism. You feel justly proud and spare a thought for those who don't drink at all, righteous souls with the plaster minds of church statues and the same vacant expressions. You make the glass last longer, running a finger idly around the rim, holding the stem nimbly between thumb and forefinger, rotating the wine in gentle swirls as you might good brandy, then drinking the stuff in one self-loathing gulp, forcing your tongue into the opening and not quite reaching the evaporating tear clinging defiantly to the bottom of the glass, another small failure anticipated. We have forced the cork in so hard it's now a devil of a job to get out. We may have to resort to the corkscrew, a guarantee that the cork will break in two, leaving half in the neck of the bottle for us to bulldoze down with our thumb. There is no more turning back. Half a bottle is worth saving. But the third glass, with the extra slugs, plunges us below the point of no return.

It is late. I have been working on my papers for hours and feel better for it. A Catholic would have the release in the confessional but few intelligent people retreat to such primeval vocations. Without knowledge life is merely the canapé before the long feast of death. As students we spent all hours discussing the meaning of existence until I reached the conclusion that the discussions were the same as existence itself, a random and absurd labyrinth that begins as we fall from the gaping wound of our mother and ends with the turbulent putrefaction of our decrepit flesh. We begin in blood and turmoil and end a small pile of waste we store in a box and lower into the gaping wound of the earth. We go from nothing to nothing and worry ourselves sick with trivia every inch of the way, gobbling up vitamins, fast walking, swimming, stretching and what's the point when the air we breathe, the food we eat, the water we drink, all are conspiring to poison our lungs, liver, kidneys, heart, blood, brain cells, immune system, hopes, dreams and our nexus to the past?

Not so long ago, I had to drive upcountry and passed close to the town where I had grown up. On the highway, there was a turn off that said 'Laughing Water' and I remembered the place from childhood. I had noticed the sign many times over the years and it always brought back the memory of that day on the river with friends when the fish had been so dense, within moments of casting your line, you could reel in your catch. It was so effortless that, young boys being more concerned with the contest than the activity, one of my companions devised a method to make the pursuit more engaging. We affixed to our rods two lines and two hooks; then three, then four. We were now able with care and luck to pull out four wriggling silver fish at once.

The sky was clear blue without cloud. Our bicycles had been thrown in a pile. The sun was warm, browning our necks and arms. We were living in the present of an endless day from an endless summer belonging less to memory than imagination. Even the fish, as if by osmosis, were in collusion with our boyish needs. Our keep nets were full. We had just reached the stage when we were yanking them out four at a time when, around the bend upstream, appeared a family of swans, a large male, a female and five cygnets in a flotilla that moved in file as if connected by hidden wires. We had layered our section of the river with bait and, with the fish responding so obligingly, the last thing we wanted was this unforeseen intrusion.

We began tossing small stones, trying to drive the swans back upstream. But they were tame creatures that would take bread from your hand with the same grudging forbearance of a beautiful woman accepting a compliment. They refused to acknowledge our threats and, staying on course, were about to pass our private spot. We were still throwing pebbles, beating the water with our rods, making seismic waves on the surface. I bent and, without searching, my hand found the perfect stone: plump, oval, flat-sided, heavy without being too heavy, a stone with some tenuous connection to me and eternity.

I weighed the stone in my palm and, though I merely threw it at the moving tableau, not a particular swan, like a Zen archer's arrow, I knew as the missile left my fingers that it would find its target. The stone hit one of the cygnets and broke its neck. The swans continued their approach as if there were a vindictive and unbreakable bond between them and me but finally, the mother turned and, steering her dead offspring with lowered beak, she guided the flotilla back in the direction from which they had come. The male followed.

My friends were quiet at first. Then they began shouting, waving their fists as if they too were connected by strings; the ties of the herd. You murderer. You killer. You termite.

"All the swans belong to the Queen. They'll put you in reform school when they find out." Rolf was there, my friend who became a photographer, hollering like a religious zealot, plotting revenge.

I left my fishing tackle on the river bank, extricated my bike from the tangle and cycled home alone, grateful to be alone. I have always been a loner, happier with my note books, my drawings, the self-conscious stories I wrote for Cristian and keep in apple boxes with old photographs, going back to them from time to time and wondering who wrote those specious fragments, who fathered that dead child? I am an architect not a writer but now, thanks to the wine, I can understand why writers become writers. It is the conclusion of all their regrets; their feelings of guilt and impotence; their remorse for each intolerable weakness; their conformity; their secret, subliminal longing for power and their paradoxical, misplaced sense of superiority. Finding few innate talents in others, they search for them within themselves, reaching for the pen in the lonely hours when there is no one to listen to their grievances; when they tire of onanism and haven't the stomach for coprophilia.

Another?

It is only my second. The body of the bottle is full. The night is a damp cloak that holds me in its embrace. I can hear tiny hands making shapes from the silence. The sun may never rise. In the humming shafts of insomnia there is something that enters with the dark, stirring the sediment below the veneer we show the neighbours and concierge. You are faced through life with the daily obstacle of being yourself and most fail. Within us all there is a mighty cry and we brood for it may merely be a whimper.

I learned how to make a confession from Mozart. Everything was plotted in his mind before he came to write the notes of his symphonies. I must have been plotting something for years. I glance through the stories written for Cristian: pirates, highwaymen, a tall prince, the most beautiful princess there ever was, and who do you think she looked like...*I pause...?*

"Like mummy?"

She has entered the bedroom with its racing car lamp and the luminous stars stuck on the ceiling. They would laugh. There is nothing to compare to the sound of a mother and child laughing, in Cristian's face a look of timelessness, the story concluded with a timely twist of fate.

I often have an urge to run away; to go simply to go. I have this vision of waking one morning and taking a train to the coast. I will leave my clothes in a folded pile on the sands and plunge into the waves, swimming in bold strokes and arriving somewhere else, a different person with a new and extrovert future. We all consist of a pocketful of lies, delusions, inventions, exaggerations, thwarted hopes and we would all like to be able to return and redraw the past.

Driving back from that last journey upcountry, I again saw the sign for Laughing Water and decided to turn off. The ramp curved between flat walls, the road narrowed and nothing I saw bore any relationship to what I remembered. I entered a complex of factory units, the glass walls reflecting empty parking lots and vacancy signs flapping in rows like beach umbrellas over an autumn beach.

I came to a halt below a large map headed Riverside Industrial Park, the rust claiming the metal surface in canny imitation of the square of land it had paved. Litter hurried by on a miscreant breeze, although the day was as warm as every day is warm. I left my jacket and walked for nearly an hour. All I saw were factories of glass and steel, the architecture of the eighties, cement roads, a few workers shambling along with that swaying, disconsolate gait they all have. I stopped one of them, a plumpish man who needed a shave. He seemed surprised by my question: Isn't there a river here, somewhere?

"River? No river here, mate. Never been a river here. Not here."

"Are you sure?"

"Definitely."

He shuffled on, proud of his inaccurate knowledge.

There had been a river at Laughing Water, a river with silver fish and white swans and once, long ago, there was a time when a squirrel could pass from the very north of the country to the southern tip without touching the ground, the trees as dense as a young head of hair, green leaf spilling on green leaf, arms enveloping tracts of black earth that had fermented through the millennia into the precious substance colonists cross mountains to seek, honest soil with a magnetic property that draws a man down to his knees so that he can press the stuff between his fingers.

It is not difficult to picture the looks on the faces of those first men who set out in search of the sea, scaling the peaks, cutting a path through the forests; brave men with patient wives and weary children who arrived on the hills and looked out upon a land laced with rivers that sang their way down to the sea shore. They would have taken off their hats, peered up at the sun, their eyes squinting as if searching for something and that something was their own good fortune in a black crescent below their fingernails. They marched down from the hills with unexpected strength and where they stopped for the night the first shelters were built.

Tribes of warriors followed. They trampled down the houses, torched the crops the pioneers had planted and settled down to raping their daughters. They united their blood with the blood of the vanquished and conceived a new race of stronger more capable men. They erected bigger houses with thicker walls and built them close for protection. The houses became a village. A wall went up to defend the village and the village became a town that unfurled into a city where

134

the farmers became merchants and their sons grew precious and scornful.

More invaders came and inscribed their names in our history books. The city walls were pulled down and higher walls were raised from the rubble. The church became a cathedral where the saints stared from stained glass windows and the first school cultivated the spires and quadrangles of the university where I dreamed my palatial dreams.

Tall elms threw parasols of shade over elegant boulevards and, outside the city walls, opposite the river, between the avenues running north from Victory Bridge and the Bridge of the Martyrs, the heath became a park and at its centre, on the island, they built a zoo for the animals adventurers brought back from their voyages to distant lands.

And people came from those same lands: immigrants and craftsmen, gypsies and inventors, Pied Pipers and princesses. And everyone said what a beautiful city it was. The years became decades, generations, centuries. The invasions became wars. But the city lived through the wars and, with the will of a mythological beast, sprouted limbs of paved roads that fondled the villages and encouraged them to become towns, and the towns stretched their wings and moved closer to the city. The forests gave way to factories and the wood was burnt to give them power. The fishing harbour became a great port and the surviving vessels that had once sailed the seven seas can be seen today, frozen in the asphalt lake below the wall where ancient mariners sit with crooked pipes surveying the sunken highway.

It was the cheer of optimism and the blare of an automobile klaxon that welcomed a century that was roaring, swinging, greedy and gay. The fields had gone but the city thrived, importing the food it had once grown and exchanging that food for machines and textiles; rubber goods and plastic goods; steel, porcelain and cement; acres of cement that covered the land where the forests had stood and took to the air in locust swarms, descending in Towers of Babel that reached for the Almighty in his outposts of our wild imaginings, endless buildings that went up and out, hiding the sky and lining the streets where children stole cars, tramps mumbled obscenities and ladies with chirpy voices wore coddled and frosty smiles.

The grand families who had once been farmers built summer houses in the hills and around those houses they erected walls trimmed with shards of glass that glinted in the sun. Within those walls they planted tropical trees in pots that decorated card table squares of lawn, havens of peace where the still was broken solely by the barking of their nervous city dogs. They rushed into the hills at the weekend and complained that too many people were rushing into the hills at the weekend. There should be controls. Politicians! They're all crooks. What's the point in voting? And they didn't. They shouted at their dogs and looked out from their picture windows as their father's fathers had done and what they saw was a portrait of stone not soil. The last of the villages in the valley had grown into towns and the towns had reached out to enmesh their fingers and become the city. And in the city something was missing and no one knew what it was. They stood in their gardens spraying dwarf pines with pesticides from cans containing compounds of CFC's that grow fangs as they rise into the air, gnawing their way through the ozone banks that protect the earth from lethal doses of ultraviolet radiation, sabotaging the food chain, molesting the oceans, raping the fish and accelerating global warming.

The last Ice Age, twelve thousand years ago, was activated by a one degree change in temperature. Since the beginning of the industrial era, the temperature has increased in some places by as much as ten degrees centigrade.

It's all here. I have notes in my notebooks, newspaper clippings going yellow with age, or sulphur deposits, a feeling of despair, even irony, when I consider that through the years I have collected these cuttings and done nothing but how could I?

I am an architect, a bureaucrat, an innocent. I am no more responsible for the catastrophe than the widows next door. There has been no time for the environment, no time for private views or thoughts beyond the obsessive universe occupied by the Lion. His demands are consuming, mesmerising, total. He devoured me. I was elevated to the dizzy heights of responsibility where I joined a team whose sole occupation was providing exactly that which at any given moment he craved.

There was never any question of his not getting what he wanted but, at the same time, he required us, his underlings, to submit to his passions and appetites in the enigmatic and exacting manner he desired. We had to bend in Aztec salute from the waist in anticipation of each new and ephemeral need and know what that need was even before the Lion knew himself. He administered his kingdom with a complex and ever-changing combination of favouritism, reproach, treachery, turmoil and the guile of a Barbary Coast buccaneer whose brutality and charm compelled women to his chamber, opponents into exile, and many to the morgue. This was the Lion's democracy, not some distorted maelstrom of individual rights and freedoms, but the

Athenian paradigm of feudal paternalism, the citizen's first duty being to their country, their first allegiance to its head.

I had been raised, let me repeat, on a simple code: *Don't Walk on the Grass*. I found myself in a delicate position, like a first son, expected to carry out our leader's every wish and then let it appear to the world, the press and to the Lion himself, that my conduct and intentions were self-motivated. The Lion spoke of his great compassion, his love of mankind, his belief in freedom and, when someone tells you something so eagerly and so often, you come to believe it, as some believe in a merciful God and I believe in my own remarkable capacity to deny by my actions the reality of what I have observed with my own eyes.

I went on study trips to Asia and Africa and what I saw, even filmed, became a mélange of trite statistics the moment I returned and entered the First Minister's office. We, as a nation, have for years been taking more from underdeveloped countries in the repayment of debt than we give in aid, and what aid we dispense is provided so that our corporations are able to secure a free hand in exploiting the natural resources of those countries. We have already depleted our own.

Somewhere in this room there is a video I made which shows a boy of about five with big eyes, a skinny body and hands raised to form a cup. A food relief vehicle has just arrived at some sordid famine camp and the boy is showing the driver he is hungry. The boy's mother, sisters and brothers are sitting in the dust with empty bellies staring into the void. The boy's father is lying at the side of the road with a pattern of holes across his chest. He is one of those sacks of waste we see on the six o'clock news in the background behind the African general riding through some dirt poor conurbation in a Jeep wearing a pale blue cravat and a Cartier wristwatch. We are warned by the newscaster that the scene may be upsetting but we sip our wine and watch anyway. Death shadows the landscape, so much death we scarcely respond.

But the little black boy with the malnourished body is captured on film where he will always be alive, anxious for life. His hands are cupped and his eyes that seem both wise and innocent focus unflinchingly on the white man unloading the sacks.

What does the white man do? Does he give an extra handful of spilled grain to the boy? Or has the boy already had his share? Is the grain for his family? Or is he driven by some selfish desire for personal survival, at the expense of others? Pushy little bleeder. If we give the extra handful to one small boy, we must give to everyone, so it's best not to give to anyone at all, the ready response of royal and rich families to worthy causes.

Imagine having to make those life and death decisions? Best be a bureaucrat. We make no decisions except those based on precedent and with no more precedents we make no decisions at all.

We sit in our living rooms with death slipping across the television screen assuming that when lots of children are dying it doesn't seem quite so appalling when your own child dies. It isn't true. For the hungry mother in the African village holding her dead infant in matchstick arms it is just as terrible as it was for Helena and me when Cristian coughed his last cough and his mouth with blue lips trembled and fell open. Helena's eyes remained dry. She was composed; serene. She wiped Cristian's mouth with a handkerchief and kissed his brow.

I stood there as if I were somewhere else, waiting for a train, perhaps, on a line that has become unprofitable and the tracks have been pulled up and the station is filled with lost tramps and old timetables. I always knew Cristian was going to die and when he died my grief was so unbearable like Helena I hid it away. I was glad it was quick and I was glad Helena's sister was out of the country. Death is a long journey taken by the living, not the dead. They shuffle off and leave us with the space they had occupied, a space Helena filled with music; me with another glass of wine. What could I have done to ease her pain? Our strength was our silence. Even Cristian went quietly. He was a quiet little boy, concluding in death the pattern of his life. He coughed mutely and left us with nothing.

Little by little, we are corrupted by reality and continue some substitute life we call life. I would have given up the Palace to have traded places. Now he had gone there was only the Palace to absorb the days. It is the worst sadness when your offspring dies before you. It makes your puny achievement futile, your universal contribution an abrupt subtraction. Cristian had been a caesarean baby. I was a modern father. I had seen him emerge with open eyes from Helena's tummy and now there was nothing left but the apple boxes full of photographs and the red bicycle in the room permanently closed.

He was five years old, the worst age to die. At five, the personality has surfaced and remains fixed, as fixed as the image of the black boy with big eyes who visits my dreams and burdens me with the vain and destitute fantasy that he still lives, one of those boys who becomes a doctor and returns to his village, a saintly man with a skinny neck and faded shirt we see on the six o'clock news, spokesman for a new famine.

Starving people are able to sit patiently hour after hour doing nothing. That boy captured on video is the exception. His mother and sisters are waiting for death. Trucks from a relief agency may appear with grain. There might be a market full of food close by. But the hungry masses do not rise up and take the food. On the contrary, they continue to do nothing.

We cannot imagine why people behave in this way, why the Jews went so passively on the long march to the gas ovens, because we are free-falling in a Prozac vacuum of complacency unable to understand what it means to be in a situation of complete hopelessness. It makes you paralysed as we are all becoming paralysed to the problems facing the planet.

The problems are too vast, too intricate, too impersonal and who cares and why care and what does it mean when you've been laid off work and the boy's been caught shop lifting and the daughter's fucking the entire neighbourhood and the washing machine's broken and the wife's a slag and there's a stone in your shoe and an ache in your back and your head and every joint and you need a beer and a holiday and just one fuck with the fourteen year old with great tits on the cover of last week's TV guide? What does it mean when you get up with black-ringed eyes, a mouth that tastes of cigarettes, cheap wine and monosodium glutamate? What does it mean when you open the newspaper and find a fresh pair of hard nipples, thighs like fertile soil, that little miracle so soft and playful you would rather be eating that for breakfast than the margarine on toast made by the fat wife with the TV dispensing its news break: War in Oombaloomba. President M'afedingledoo defies UN. Bleary eyes. Restless nights. Nightmares.

They fall from high buildings. They climb tall towers and can't climb down again. They peer into lift shafts and climb spiral staircases to tubes that funnel to infinity. They see spiders, giant crabs and magazine pages that flutter like autumn leaves and on every one there's something out of reach: beautiful homes, beautiful women, beautiful men, new cars, new laptops, holidays in Java, perfect lips, perfect tits, out of reach, beyond touch, beyond the clasp of grasping fingers.

They are trapped. I am trapped. We're all trapped. Trapped by our narrow minds, scarcity of imagination, our plebeian, poverty-stricken lack of courage. Trapped in boxes and coffins and in spaces that fill with flies, the walls pressing in, the ceiling coming down, the sky lowering like a filthy blanket. They get up with eye sockets that burn, throats crawling with dead insects, and make their nightmares come true: climbing towers, leaping from elevator shafts, throwing themselves under morning trains clutching tinfoil sandwiches, jumping from bridges and flyovers and into the uncertainties of another new day; rising to the chimes of a brutal alarm, sinking into black coffee and cigarettes, or yoga and yoghurt, vitamin pills, weight control pills, nerve pills, depression pills, boredom pills, happy pills, the same as the children but not the same. We are not crazed by energy, ecstasy and passion. But a quiet, gradual, crumbling pessimism.

Two facts we at the Palace have never revealed: euthanasia is commonly practised; suicides double annually.

Such is city life. Bright lights and boredom. Runaways in cardboard beds. Bag ladies with swollen ankles and shiny eyes. The jobless with their despondency. Foreigners photographing it all. The old reeling with timeless futility between the parked cars and running children, staring at the ground, the takeaway food cartons, archipelagos of dogshit and the nodding, confident pigeons: vermin of the air, as the Lion calls them. Creeping through supermarkets complaining, reminiscing, not listening, standing in lines and waiting. Waiting for traffic. Waiting for a letter. Waiting for a visit. Waiting for the telephone to ring. If there is a God above He has a rare sense of humour saving old age for the worst time in life when we are old and waiting, sitting in miserable slums staring through unwashed windows, listening to the hum of the highway, the drone of the television, their own voices whispering to mute and sour pets: goldfish in bowls, flightless canaries, parsimonious cats and nervous city dogs that leave their marks along the avenues of flickering street lamps, over the wheels of cars, in the doorways of shops closed for the night, on the sacks of waste where people eat and sleep and drink themselves to oblivion; guard dogs, blind dogs, dogs with diarrhoea, loose-legged puppies bought by fathers for children they don't know and can't support, snappy runts with tight-bottomed ladies, killer dogs howling from empty rooms. It is a city of dogs. Famed for its dogs. Famed for its cathedral where the saints stare from stained glass windows, the water is boiled or bought in bottles, where the deadly fumes have coagulated into a dark miasmic canopy and the complex of the Palace of Democracy is the most substantial architectural undertaking since the erection of the Great Wall of China and shares with it both the distinction of being visible from the moon and a significant parallel in its method of construction.

I should rest my mind. Oil my throat.

Twelve

That's better. Like the Greeks, one does well paying homage to the grape. I read *The Grapes of Wrath* with particular interest and once, while dipping into a novel by Mario Vargas Llosa, work momentarily forgotten, the Lion entered and shook his head with the awe one shows a man who juggles knives in a blindfold.

"Another talent, I see," he said without humour and there was something in the tone of his voice that made me more despondent than usual.

That evening, after a couple of drinks, I did something rather astonishing: I wrote the name of the nation's leader on a scrap of paper which I sealed in an airtight jar and banished to the frozen wastes of the deep-freeze, this pagan deed like sticking pins in a voodoo doll to activate the downfall of one's nemesis.

As you know, he suffered no visible decline and, later in the year, when we buried Cristian, I made a point of removing the jar and throwing it away.

I studied the Lion across the graveside, his hair like a flaming torch below a leaden sky, and my mind, sullied as it is by the paradox, by the power of opposites, clouded further with a terrible vision of the great wheel of cause and effect spinning round with my own malevolent longings reshaped into tragedy. The cliché was right: we are our own worst enemy. We yearn to swim but, as Proust realised, keep one foot planted on the ground.

There are biologists who believe each evil thought directed at another, whether the action behind it is carried out or not, creates a 'protein' we bear with us forevermore. A brain cell is infused with that thought and, like a birthmark; it cannot be eradicated, even if later events compel us to modify our opinion. If we grow to admire the despised person, the original cell with its spiteful programme and the new cell will co-exist in a state of mild confusion that germinates into schizophrenia, dementia and, if it wasn't so depressing, would certainly make us depressed. I have no way of knowing how many brain cells I have contaminated with Helena's sister but, if the scientists are on course, my future will be as the past, future lives unliveable.

She arrived back from somewhere, disappointed to have missed the burial, or missed the chance of standing alongside FM dressed in black, his favourite colour, and insisted on dragging Helena off to pray for Cristian's soul. I found the whole thing nauseating and must have shown my feelings by my expression.

"You never cease to surprise me, Tomas. Don't you care about your own child?" Stella said.

"When he was alive, my dear. Now, it's a bit late."

She glanced at Helena. "You see. He's always attacking me. Every time I speak, I'm crucified by his vile tongue," she said and turned on me, beaming: "You know, you will find in Heaven exactly what you anticipate. Those who expect nothing enter a vacuum where they encounter nothing."

I said nothing. I felt nothing. Helena stood there like a willow tree confronting an axe murderer. Demons were entering with the morning light. Stella was on her feet, gathering her cigarettes. She seemed oddly at ease with our grief, impatient to be practical, her hands clasped in front of her, propping up her astonishing breasts so

146

that she appeared to be posing for something mildly pornographic. Unlike Helena, an ectomorph charged with diffuse nervous energy, Stella is an endomorph, a fussy little blonde with a bottom like a pair of down cushions and the annoying capacity of finding time to meet friends at airports and visit twice weekly her ageing mother.

Being unmarried, she had a strong sense of the past and discovered never-ending pleasure in recounting monotonous and inconsequential episodes from an unremarkable childhood, her themes the interlacing tiles of an elaborate and constantly unfolding mosaic that, like a recurring nightmare, brings to mind my lifetime's work. No matter was too trifling to reach resolution. The tile was eternally there, ready at all times to be gathered anew and placed elsewhere in the pattern, instituting the long, complicated necessity of rearranging the configuration into a new but similar pattern. Everything that had ever been discussed would be discussed again. Every decision ever made back to infancy, back to the coddled soup of the womb, would have to be reassessed, and every decision made as a result of that decision would have to be picked over as the bleached white bones of a pterodactyl have been picked over by the mammoth, prehistoric vultures, the rats, roaches and palaeontologists wearing rubber gloves and steel-rimmed glasses. There were not sufficient hours in the day to discuss all that was, all that had ever been, and everything that now resulted as a corollary of that and every conversation, and that which would have to be done, changed, rearranged and reconsidered in the aftermath of the ultimate but ephemeral conclusion.

I could go on.

I drove through the mute wilderness of an autumn Sunday, Stella occupying the centre of the rear seat where her blue eyes scrutinised

147

me in the interior mirror with the possessed satisfaction of a child with a computer game. Stella had a large, sensual mouth and, as it unhinged, my fleeting glance in the mirror made me think of those snakes that devour their prey whole and spend weeks on digestion.

"I only want what's best for everyone," she said, placing a hand on my shoulder. "You just don't seem to understand what I'm saying."

"No, dear, but I understand what you're trying to say," I answered.

She sat back wearing a martyred, if uncertain look and we continued in silence until we reached the Old Quarter where the cathedral rose over the slums like a shipwreck on a wind swept beach, this architectural orphan a symbol of the Lion's grudging respect for the power more than the message of the Church.

Stella closed the door with a slam. "You should come with us. It might put you in better humour."

"Only two things are worthy of humour, my dear: human fornication and evacuation."

Helena shook her head.

"You beast," Stella cried drawing breath. "Your poor mama had rare insight when she named you Tomas. You Doubter," she cried with a fine spray of spit, turning and marching off, her breasts guiding her into the cathedral as the bass drum leads a parade, Helena following like a cloud of perfume turned acrid, tainting her features, as bitterness sours the soul. She accompanied her sister to please her sister, wrongly believing her sister was accompanying her to please her.

I surveyed the cathedral's crumbling façade. There was a painted sign showing a thermometer with dates and numbers marking donations to the restoration fund. It had been there, rising slowly, for as long as I could recall. I was wondering what to do with the red bicycle that glinted malevolently in Cristian's room, the racing car lamp, the Teddy bear with scratched glass eyes and a passing resemblance to Anton.

Prostitutes hurried by with shopping bags and swollen faces. I thought about taking a walk, to see if I could find the Wise Monkey, but couldn't be bothered. Death does that.

I stared through the windscreen at the thermometer, at the yellow sky. Helena and Stella going to morning prayer put me in mind of Sisyphus rolling a rock up a precipice. They were searching for God in a maze of distorting mirrors. It had taken forty million years for the first reptiles to slither from the slurp and sprout limbs. In a single century, the lifespan of herdsmen in the Caucasus, we have filled the atmosphere with a substance that eats stone. It was like a miracle. We were at the end of the Christian era; the end of history. It was Sodom and Gomorrah and who gives a damn? Genesis 19:24 promises every ending's just a beginning, verses I remember from Bible Classes. I have a marvellous memory for the obscure and irrelevant. If I could live my life again, I'd become a chess player, using my memory to study the moves of the masters, emulating them, joining them. Life is a parable for the motions of chess: a violent confrontation performed within an arena of striking contrasts among men of diverse yet limited capability.

I could hear organ music. The sky was hung with Gothic clouds. Like the smell on my hands, the car reeked of smoke. Stella smoked incessantly, carelessly, lighting each cigarette from the brazier of the last, flicking ash about her like rice at a wedding, like the data that pours from the Ministry of Railways and Science. She smoked, not for pleasure, but politics, for the party. Smoking, we had finally proved, without a molecule of doubt, and all doctors agree, is good for your health. You can read the recommendation on the packets. And there is no pollution in our city. And no homelessness. And there is no sickness except hypochondria: the disease of the lazy and the liberals.

"We have the cleanest air in the civilised world," Stella had announced out of the blue that morning, running her hand over Helena's hair in a gesture I had never liked. Stella smiled a good deal; listened to old people when they were talking. She had about her an air of radiant good will. But beneath the breasts and blue frock ticked a mechanical device that could be set as easily as a time bomb. Like the readers of certain newspapers, it wasn't hard to programme Stella to believe anything. She was a Reform League activist who had found the meaning of life in the party doctrine and, as with all extremists, she hated the Opposition with a fetish beyond the call of human dignity. The contamination of the air we breathed, like the destruction of the rain forests, was merely the propaganda of Evergreen *liberals,* a word that on Stella's tongue conjured visions of something repulsive, sacrilegious, as rank smelling as jimsonweed.

As a civil servant, I refrained from occupying a political position and, frankly, was wearied by the carping, apocalyptic theories of the Evergreen Alliance. I had never thought that much about the environment until Cristian died and now he was dead, I didn't care much about anything at all. Let the people of the world get on with destroying themselves. Why should I worry? My world lay about me in ruins like the ruined slums around the cathedral.

150

"The Lion is a Saint," Stella often said and, at that moment, I couldn't help wondering if she were right. My black magic in the bowels of the deep-freeze had harmed no one but myself. There was no Almighty to tip doom down on our First Minister. His path to Paradise is as straight as a Roman road and, on arrival, Peter will greet him like a small piece of granite returning to the Mother Rock, his seed generously spread.

Even Stella had performed this personal service. She had moved from the Ministry of Agriculture and Pensions to FM's office where, as a secretary, like the multitudes before her, she had travelled in our leader's wake taking notes for the girls in the computer pool to send to the various departments. It should be made clear that Stella was not the Lion's *poison*, as you might say, bearing those extra kilos fore and aft, but had undoubtedly arrived a confirmed virgin and, for a virgin, even the Lion made sacrifices.

She had been quickly discarded (more quickly than most, as a matter of fact) but entered what we called *The Clitorati*, that legion of party workers who went to church, expressed strong feelings about foreigners and occupied that part of the Reform League where the women enjoyed flagellation and the men tight uniforms. The League for Stella was a mission and from her I have learned an important lesson: beware of conservative women who speak of politicians with goo-goo eyes.

I have a note in an old diary: You can judge a person's character by the way they treat books.

Stella broke the spines and folded the pages and creased the covers, returning cherished novels to the coffee table where they would lie like bloated fish washed up on the shores of a silent sea.

There. That's a few more abused brain cells to worry about.

Thirteen

Let us get back to the Great Wall of China.

What an interesting structure it is. If you have the money and a good pair of walking boots, go to the nearest travel agent and book a tour. The best time to go is in the spring, when the orange blossom fills the trees. Stand at the top of one of the look-out towers outside the old capital and amaze yourself when you see the edifice reaching out to claim the past and the future.

It is not generally known but the Great Wall was built in separate, often isolated sections, each section with an army of workers under the control of a lord mason who, after a decade of duty, could admire the result of his toil in a completed masterpiece of stone. The assumption that the wall would keep the Mongol hordes from invading the country was more important than the reality that its length was too great for it to be defended. The wall's purpose was to unite the people behind a common cause (a mainly imagined and overstated enemy) while the mandarins persisted with the Chinese arts of high living, high etiquette and the custody of power.

I was made a lord mason. I moved into a government office with the arrogance of one who assumes he has been chosen by fate, a feeling that must occur to musical prodigies and the children of the rich. On the wall behind my desk I displayed a doctorate laden with wax seals and, just as woodworm leaps into holes left by a predecessor, I began to pursue a path along a tunnel lit by the enlightened thinking of the day. The criticism that had first greeted the decision to build the new Palace began to fade, leaving merely the residue: the pejorative pentangle that, as with the traditions we cling to most fervently, had shed the umbilical cord of my blueprints and was living a life of its own. There were new disasters to trouble the good citizenry: our national soccer team had been beaten in a cup match by Oombaloomba and, that same week, the First Minister had marched out of a luncheon attended by world leaders on a point of protocol; who in their right mind would serve vanilla ice cream without chocolate sauce? The subtlety of his intellect was audacious. Clever reviewers in their Sunday columns would be ripping out clawfuls of hair as they played the snakes and ladders of his irony. The more the Lion roared, the more his countrymen believed he had their interests at heart, the more they accepted the Palace of Democracy. If you want people to believe in something, it must be certain. What is more certain than cement being poured?

While I was still wallowing in that brief period of callow vanity, it occurred to me that man needs more than a mere wage packet for him to set off for work each day. He needs to see something ensuing from his labours and, like boys with fishing poles, he is most contented in the perpetual angst of competition.

With FM's reticent approval and, taking a lesson from the ancient Chinese, I created work gangs under capable foremen and dispatched them to the five far-flung corners of the common. While the Palace was rising beside the lake at the centre of the site, squads of navvies were digging the footings that would enclose the complex in mock marble walls and engineers were constructing the monorail connecting the helicopter pads, logically placed at the two extreme points below the park's northern peak.

Even as the iron rods coated in titanium were sliding into moulds and the moulds were being filled with cement, I was moving through my virtual reality programme throwing up additions and extensions, a burgeoning maze of connecting corridors, polyurethane tunnels, ornate bridges, interlacing pentahedrons of intricate and essential structures: a library, museums, art galleries, ministry towers, barracks, sports stadia, a prison, the king's new residence and the coliseum of living history where we recreated the story of our city from the days of our forebears to the ultimate panel containing the Lion and his courtiers outside the Palace, a scene where I was able to pay tribute to the architects who built the tombs of the pharaohs by placing Helena and myself peering charmingly from the crowd gathered in the background.

Everything, as you know, follows the five-sided leitmotiv of the original and extends in dilating units like a spider's web. The open courtyards running between the outer buildings were not established as an outcome of pressure from the Evergreens, as they claimed, but were motivated by a committee decision that encouraged me to emulate the Caliphs of Moorish Spain, the temple groves of Heliopolis, the orangeries of Italy, the Hanging Gardens of Babylon and, with the sound of helicopters reminding me of bombs forever falling in the Lion's favourite movies, I was inspired to recreate the peace garden at Hiroshima with seas of raked sand graced by twisted roots of bakelite driftwood and bonsai willows that nurture exotic shadows in the glow of the halogen lights.

I did suggest importing some Orientals to do the raking but the First Minister's eye-brows enmeshed across his brow like ivy on a country house, impeding the light of intimate discussion. It was a minor point and, generally, I had unlimited autonomy as the head of the department, leading a staff divided equally between people chosen by me and those engaged by the Lion, women like Stella, who took notes at meetings, and broad-shouldered men with large hands and a remarkable ability to get things done.

While the courtyards were being built, it was the Minister for Arts and Sewage who proposed employing native artists to create a garden of statues to adorn the pentagon adjoining his Ministry. In the wake of the condemnations that had first greeted the government's decision to honour democracy with its unique shrine, the fresh offensive was anticipated and ignored.

The detractors rounded on the project with sharpened wit ('A Surreal Graveyard,' ran one headline). But, disregarding the criticism, the sculptures were laid out according to the desires expressed at committee. As ever, we bow to the tenets of democracy and the will of the majority they ultimately represent.

Anton Cesar was outraged that his avant-garde installations had not been selected and made a point of climbing the two flights of stairs from his apartment with its lingering scent of Bulgarian champagne to visit me at home. Yes, he would have a glass of wine. Just the one.

"You understand, Tomas, it's not that I care, per se. I have a reputation. So many, so very many, of the nation's artists, as is well known, learned their craft in the very department of which I am the head."

"Politicians," I said, shrugging so liberally I almost spilled my drink.

He pulled at his pointed beard. With the round spectacles he pushed up his nose and the enlarged paunch girdered by a striped waistcoat, Anton had grown to resemble those jobbing actors employed as elves in department stores at Christmas.

"You've chosen Gabriel Latour! That's what they're saying," he said. "The man's an idiot. A nincompoop. A monster. Painted cubes. It's a mockery. All art is derivative..."

"Indeed."

"...but in derivation you take a step forward," he went on, approaching me in his eagerness to demonstrate. "Latour has taken a step into God knows where, into the abyss. Into a black hole."

I refilled his glass before he stepped back to rest his arm on the mantel, his head immediately next to a Latour abstract he had failed to notice, the conspiracy of place, painting and subject adding a vaudevillian air to the proceedings.

"You have to do something, Tomas."

"I will do my best," I said. "It's such a problem being surrounded by philistines."

"Indeed."

We drank our wine. The sun was a vivid shade of orange. I was almost in a good mood.

The final selection for the garden of statues would turn out to be a committee decision over which I had no influence. I did mention Anton's name during the debate but the Minister of Arts and Sewage had his own agenda and my neighbour failed to make the short list.

In later years, I occasionally heard Anton boast that his work *had* been chosen but *he* had refused permission for its use, a pardonable invention under the circumstances.

As for the lake, there have been sufficient words written on the subject to furnish the new library; I make this brief footnote:

We had intended to keep the lake. Of course. There was never any question of that. But, you know, it had become a terrible eyesore, the green fungus carpeting the surface, the litter washed up on the shores. People in the dead of night were dumping refrigerators and old sofas in the shallows. The bottle banks and newspaper bins were never properly serviced and, to no one's surprise, we discovered it had been the responsibility of an enterprise owned by the brother-in-law of the former First Minister. The corruption of the previous administration had been so extreme, so extravagant, it could be compared to the labyrinth at Knossos; years in the making and still more years in being exposed by the assiduous archaeologists of the national press, a number of whom were named each year in the Lion's Democracy Day Honours.

I went by the lake every day on my journey to the Palace. Helena sometimes accompanied me, braving the air, and was present that morning when we literally stumbled upon the horrid results of someone's negligence: the ducks, geese, moorhens, tame peacocks, the squirrels that begged for nuts and the disdainful white swans that took bread from the palm of your hand would be taking bread no longer. All were dead, lying where they had fallen among the little green scribbles left like signatures by the geese.

"What have they done? They're killing everything," Helena said. She had turned pale. "We must get away. It's evil here."

"It's the same everywhere."

"Is it?"

"I don't know."

I could hear mechanical diggers, the grind of traffic, a helicopter coming in to land. Helena had taken my arm. She started to shake me, suddenly, violently.

"Tomas, Tomas. For God's sake, wake up. Look around you."

I looked around me.

I remembered the song of the saws; small boys crying *timber*. The trees had gone. That vast, empty space belonged to me. Yes me. From where we stood, I had an unobstructed view of my creation. The Palace of Democracy rose up before us, a black monolith without shadows or shine, the mouldings imperceptible in the dull light, the windows with the same air of serene mystery as the eyes of the swans and squirrels at our feet. The sketches on my drawing board were real, tangible, a mirage come to life, the domes, towers and spires piercing the dust yellow sky, the great resin Gods gazing out from the five façades, as awesome as the sets in a film by Ridley Scott or Cecil B De Mille. I had made the largest piece of art the world has ever seen. To Michelangelo, Rembrandt, Velásquez, Duchamp and Ramses I, II and III, you can add the name: Tomas Sala.

It was heady stuff.

The Evergreen Alliance would claim that the tragedy had been caused by the discharge of antibiotics, contraceptive pills and chemotherapy drugs with human sewage, the waste leaking into the underground channels that fed the lake. How ridiculous! Such incidents may occur in other countries. They do not occur in our own.

It was a natural disaster due to the fungus, as the commission of inquiry submitted in its report. The debate went on for more than a year; the smell a good deal longer. It even damaged the League in local elections although, as the Lion made clear, just as judges selected by government remain independent in their court rooms, the commission had been independent and its account of the facts altogether objective.

With their steady diet of household refuse and takeaway food, the city pigeons were curiously immune from the virus, in the same way that the modest ant is thought to be so well conceived it would be able to survive a nuclear deluge without changing form. The pigeons, impatient to fill the available space left by the departed wild life, began to multiply as tenaciously as a fascist state preparing for war, moving in clouds like the planes over Guernica, dropping explosives on the five domes decorating the Palace roof and driving the Lion into the cellars of a rare depression that impoverished his love life and carved into his face a portrait of heart-rending melancholia. He took the invasion as a personal assault on his honesty, authority, credibility, his position as the duly elected First Minister. He became a stage lion with a thorn in its paw.

In answer to his despair, we formed the Pigeon Committee. A National Pigeon Controller was employed and radio broadcasts, following the weather report, tracked their movements. The pigeons continued to roam the Old Quarter where some people kept them as pets, and still more began to do so. But, within the Palace grounds, the Controller's marksmen were ordered to shoot interlopers on sight. There have been accidents; that child that's always mentioned. The positive side, however, was seeing the Lion with shiny eyes staring up at the glass domes above the debating chamber when he materialised unexpectedly with words of advice, departing just as suddenly with short rapid steps to continue the innumerable affairs that fill the hours of a government head.

The Lion did not concern himself with the daily minutiae of committee although his ultimate approval on all matters was imperative.

One issue he did follow closely was the need for an animal sanctuary. Many of the animals in the old zoo on the island had perished in the epidemic and, once the lake had been drained, the reclaimed land was ideal for the new Ministry of Sports and Defence. The First Minister prowled around the five walls of the room, his hands locked behind his back, his ears cocked, registering every word that was said. Someone who had just returned from overseas was relating the story of a tea party attended by costumed chimpanzees and the anecdote had become so long-winded the Lion stopped in his tracks, beat his chest, and gave an almighty bellow.

"Bugger the apes. What about elephants and rhinos. They're what I call animals."

"I agree wholeheartedly," said the Minister of Animal Affairs.

"That settles that," the First Minster said and hurried from the chamber taking his new secretary with him, just eighteen, she had been praised by her boss in a magazine interview for the uncanny speed of her shorthand.

The Animal Minister, a jolly autodidact who had made a fortune importing cheap porcelain - he wore a miniature bidet on a gold chain around his neck - ordered further research that revealed the distressing fact that, while the jungles of Africa and Asia were being ruthlessly cleared for cultivation by American agri-corporations, the elephant, rhinoceros, the lion, hippopotamus and giraffe had ceased to roam the wilds except in preserves designated for photo-safaris. Everyone on the committee considered the situation scandalous and we set out like Noah to improve matters by importing two of each of the threatened species.

We had already decided to keep a family of zebra when the Lion discovered the quagga and developed a rare admiration for this sturdy beast that had been hunted on the South African veldt for hides regarded as ideal as grain sacks. Only three quaggas still remained and they had long undergone the craft of the taxidermist. We managed at great cost to acquire one of these stuffed specimens from the natural history museum in a country whose name escapes my memory and the genetic engineers engaged on the project regularly tell us that the day when a baby quagga can be seen roaming free in the First Minister's private pentangle is fast approaching.

I am not sure how they managed to cross breed the goats, llamas, horses and deer to produce the unicorn and, though the body is somewhat heavy and the horn upon the creature's forehead is as yet a modest growth, while optimism endures, we must praise the skill of the biologists, not our labour in the debating halls of bureaucracy.

The interminable discussions, often over minor points, did become tiresome but one had to remain earnest in their endeavours. I remember one drawn out meeting on a stuffy afternoon during the animal crisis when the Animal Minister, one Maurice Gigot, suggested we breed the carousel horse. We all laughed at his droll sense of the absurd and he went home that warm evening with the feeling that life was treating him with special care.

We find it easy to be contented when we have something to look forward to and, though these joyful periods are eclipsed when new pleasures seem dim on the horizon, the Minister saw his humour as the path, leading straight to the Environment Ministry with a seat beside the Lion. A ready wit is the short cut to popularity although, being the twin mask to tragedy, comedy can produce puzzling effects.

By the time the jolly porcelain importer had arrived at the Ministry the following day, his office had been erased. The units, seamlessly joined in interchangeable pentangles are, like play bricks, just as easy to slide apart as they are to slot together. The desk, files, books, the paintings on the walls, the trolley with bottles, the adjoining office bejewelled with a personal assistant passed down by the Lion. Everything had ceased to exist as if it had never existed.

That same day, I found Maurice Gigot staring at me from the morning paper. Below the 140-point Bodoni Bold headline: TAX FRAUD, was the shocking revelation that the Minister had failed to keep proper books and had systematically cheated the treasury out of millions.

"If the fat cats imagine they can get away with it they can think again," a government spokesman told a press conference on the palace steps. "While the good honest people of this wonderful country are paying their taxes, the First Minister will not tolerate knaves and swindlers who try to take advantage of what I can only describe as the most liberal and honest system in the world, one, I need not add, that is envied throughout the world."

The Animal Minister, confirming to many his guilt, claimed in a telephone interview from Paris that his life had been threatened by Reform League thugs and he had been forced to flee. His empire was

163

a house of cards that soon came tumbling down. He lost his money. His children were removed from school. His wife filed for divorce and Maurice Gigot flung himself from the top floor of a hotel leaving a brief note that said: I'm sorry, I didn't mean it.

The details were fully reported in the press although, when the man's name was mentioned at a conference soon after his suicide, the Lion was unable to recall his former Minister of Animal Affairs and rectified this oversight by inviting the man's widow to a private meeting at his office where, in his inimitable way, Madame Gigot departed a new woman.

This was the mark of the Lion's munificence. He enjoyed giving the gift of a picture frame containing a photograph of himself. He was intrigued by the notion of generosity, as he liked the idea of reading books. But they were concepts that struck him as being foolish and vaguely sinister. Like Stalin, gratitude had not been programmed into his DNA.

He described himself as *lion-hearted*, an image he fostered by castigating himself for his benevolence, citing as verification the fact that he alone of all world leaders had established the dream of full employment. The League had removed the sordid crutch of welfare and had provided instead a wide-ranging series of grants covering all manner of subjects. Those who did not qualify - the majority, it now appears - had no soul-destroying hand out to cling to and were compelled into a state of dignity among the numerous unskilled pursuits formerly filled by foreign workers, most of whom had no resident's permits and had entered the country under the laissez-faire immigration policy maintained by the previous régime.

The finance for the new scholarships was available from the cash saved on education and the spirits of many good citizens rose to levels of pure ecstasy when they could proudly tell their neighbour that the music beating down the adjoining wall was not their son's idle recreation but his scrupulous meditation upon a home university course. The voters quickly appreciated the system's advantages although, being another controversial issue, it only found its way on to the statute books at the expense of the entire commission that had first drafted the proposal.

Over the years, everyone I have ever known on every commission has gone, moved on, retired, died, eloped with a fortune, disappeared in disgrace. One never noticed at the time because the turnover was staggered and there were always more ambitious civil servants and deputies climbing the ladder to the Lion's den. I have endured, not because I had never been elected to office, and not because the Lion feels some latent affection for me. Great men, refraining from such foibles, require an ever-changing audience rather than constant scrutiny.

Put simply, it seems the First Minister recognised in me the lack of any desire to thrive at the expense of others, a characteristic he finds both amusing and inconceivable. He spoke often of his belief in tradition and continuity. I am its symbol. The Lion can point at me and say, "Look, this is my architect. He has been with me for twenty years. He has a beautiful wife; her coldness intrigues me. I attended his son's funeral. He is a private drinker with a soggy brain like a filing cabinet filled with the minutes of a million committees."

Within a year of my appointment as Chief Architect I had already become a committee man: part human, part robot, part parrot.

I would rush home from the office, eager to tell Helena all the petty things that had been said and done.

"The Minister of Highways and Parking wants to pave the river," I remember telling her. "Can you imagine anything so stupid?"

"Yes," she said.

"Yes?" I repeated.

She was playing the cello and I had a momentary vision of the notes as a swarm of butterflies hovering about her hair. She stopped and they disappeared.

"Hasn't the minister just built a house beside the river?"

"Yes..."

"Work it out, Tomas."

She continued playing, but stopped again. "Let's go to the Indian restaurant. I'm dying for something spicy."

I went to change. I thought about what Helena had said. We, too, had just bought a house in the hills. I was in the process of building an ornamental wall to enclose a flower garden and choosing each stone (yes, *stone*) seemed vitally significant, as choosing curtains and colours for the nursery had infinite importance to Helena.

Five years had quickly elapsed. I was confronting the hurdle of being thirty; Helena was in the middle months of being pregnant. She was happy. We both were. I had got into the habit at night of resting my head on the arch of her stomach and listening to the morse code of approaching feet. "Daddy. Daddy."

I could hear him coming.

"A boy or a girl?" she asked.

"A boy," I replied.

"We can have a computer scan and make sure."

"There's no need. I can hear his voice."

Helena ran her padded fingertips down the long cello neck of my arm. "What's he saying?"

"Daddy. Daddy."

"Daddy. Daddy," she repeated, testing the words. "Mummy. Mummy."

In the flower garden I planted bougainvillaea. It bloomed briefly like Latin women and then began to fade. Its leaves withered and its limbs clung in vain to the wall, gnarled and naked, hanging on like the jade tree on the corner of my desk, a plant that reminds me so much of me I adore its endurance and detest it for just the same reason. The little tree is a traveller from another time or place or planet. Its leaves are curled and bulbous, scornful of neglect, thirst, sulphur fumes, the dark places in this room forever beyond the reach of the plump bodied lamps that occupy the side tables like fat ladies in small elevators; gloom deserts where dustballs and cockroaches go about their nocturnal quests like old men who need no excuse to go out in the late hours to visit their lover. The jade tree is my lover. We have known each other so long sex is no longer an issue. I never bring her gifts. I put no water in the pot and feed her randomly on the dregs from bottles of bitter wine. She is an alcoholic.

Fourteen

I have managed to ease my way down the bottle. The night grows warmer; darkness thickens. Time never sleeps. It races. At ten we look back at being nine and it is ten percent of your life. At twenty a year is five percent. At fifty it is two percent, so brief we glance over our shoulder and it has gone. Every year seems shorter and is shorter. We start to confuse habit with truth; routine with reality; boredom with apathy. The surprise we can tolerate far more than the stagnant grind of the predictable. We wait away our lives dreaming of catching a glimpse of something remarkable, something that tells us all the waiting has been worthwhile, and now the telephone is ringing, so sudden and extraordinary the wine in my bloodstream has turned to glass.

It rang four times.

It is the indefinable sound that awakes us from a nightmare, four double rings that invade the stale hour with a surreal, ambivalent air, the sound caressing the silence like the faint cry whispering through the night's interminable still: Cristian's voice, an echo that journeys on and on and will only rest when those who remember him have gone.

"Daddy. Daddy."

"Mummy. Mummy."

It rang four times and I gazed at the machine as if I were a statue in a museum; an extinct bird contemplating an invisible sheet of perspex.

The hands of the clock are preparing their midnight rendezvous. I am unable to recall what part of time Paris occupies, the past or the future. I sit in vigil over the bottle of wine, anticipating the morning headache as the next step on the wheel of a treadmill.

I listened to the ringing as if the telephone was in another building and I was passing a window vainly wondering if it could be for me. We wait for friends and wives and lovers to call and when they call we have nothing to say. Out there, in the wilderness, there is someone with a message that begins with a pause that is followed by a sigh, and concludes with the solitary word:

"Tomas!"

Then a click.

The answering machine faithfully records every breath: Pause. Sigh. Tomas. Click.

She speaks with sorrow and impatience. I can see her blue marble eyes, the pale bruises in the fissures of her cheeks, her long, ungainly limbs.

"Tomas!"

Her tone is irritated but bears a maternal affection that is pervasive, timeless, ubiquitous. We will always be together in some remote speck of substance chipped from our souls and fastened as one. We share something: the two of us standing over a half-sized coffin beside a half-sized grave. A red bicycle in a sealed and silent room. First steps. First words. Shared laughter. The first look of a boy who emerged with open eyes from the gaping wound of your stomach, festooned in a tangle of grey and bloody tubes. The nurse wrapped him in a white cloth and when she gave him to me he gazed into my eyes with the querulous expression of the savant being confronted by something charming and ridiculous. The next day, Cristian had begun the long sleep of infancy, but there were those few moments, peculiar to caesarean births, when the fully formed being, secure in its watery cosmos, passes into our world, a mature foetus that is not yet a baby, a few brilliant seconds after it departs from the umbilical cord and stares into the future, and those seconds belong to me.

Helena is calling. She is sleepless and alone, sitting up in bed below a dim light with a novel half read and no recollection of the words that covered the last five pages. Her mind wanders secluded paths, winding around little tufts of memory, brittle and dry like dunes in the desert.

"Tomas!"

The replay is immediate. I can feel the pause, detect the sigh, remember the long suffering look of undying futility.

"Tomas!"

She was a woman unable to deceive. Her thoughts were in the orbs of her mausoleum eyes, in the lines that touched her brow like creases in fine parchment, in the spectres that strayed across her cheeks like the shadows of clouds over a hillside. We would make love with Mozart in the background, her arms and legs in a dance around my own as if we were an octopus wriggling on the spikes of a trident caught by the fishermen on the coast of Greece. We had watched them beating out the black ink that sullies the taste when the creature is cooked, the guts staining the rocks red as they cleaned them and, bereft of intestines and brains, still they stir like the four arms and four legs of lovers who have sweated and shed their anïs-and-water essence on the white sheets always tightly tucked by your strong fingers. I loved your slender limbs, your fragile shoulders, your belly that was never flat again after Cristian was born, your back that hollowed into two shallow pools, the skeleton keys of your spine like the saxophone I always imagined I would learn to play. Your hair grew shorter with the years, more boyish, but your eyes with their theatre of emotions remained the same pale blue of placid skies at summer's end, the purple blue of heliotropes turning their heads to the sunrise, the blue of faded blue jeans you are too fond of to throw away. When we made love your nipples changed from pink to violet. In your arms I was the child you would lose. You were the sister I imagined and never had. Your body was the forgotten landscape returned to after many years: everything changed yet familiar like the faces of my parents who had the good grace to run a hose from the exhaust of their car through the window and, the garage doors closed, they drifted into oblivion. The pleasant man at the crematorium suggested keeping them together in the same urn. People like that sort of thing.

You stretched like a cat. Your body was two bodies: the adolescent, not fully formed body of your thin shoulders and protruding collar bones, and the woman's body lined in ivory trails lit by the twilight. I cherished those lines, the filigree basket of your pubic hair which I stroked as if beneath my hand I nursed a unicorn. You made me believe beauty was an inherent quality. People who were not beautiful outside I assumed were not beautiful inside and created their ugliness in the vats of ugly souls. It was hard to believe Stella had sprung from the same loins. She made me wary of people who went to church. I was suspicious of men in business suits and

171

became one. We are all prey to the paradox; victims of irony. We are all absurd.

I realised I fostered an uncommon strain of schizophrenia that day when I watched the trees being felled in the park, then crossed the river by the Victory Bridge, climbed the steps to my office, and began designing a new pentangle that would stand in the place where the trees had stood. I would decorate the site with dwarf pines that grow in pots. Like you, Helena, I am two people: the sober architect and the cloistered drinker who finds Anton Cesar's satyr features among the watermarks above the bed where you would lie like a translucent lake reflecting secrets in the moon of your timeless expression.

I will return your call. But later.

I am on my feet, standing erect like a good homo sapien, splashing down the last lap of wine, acrid now as if to confirm my conviction that nothing turns out as we had hoped. A pessimist, it's said, is just a well informed optimist. The last drop feeds the jade tree, a money tree they say in China.

There my dear, are you happy now?
Why of course you're still beautiful.
We'll always be together.
And I love you, too.

The night has cooled. From my balcony I see nebulous flares like pulsing sores above the Old Quarter. The sound of my breathing is consumed in the sky tides of infinite sulphur. The widows are dreaming unimaginable dreams. I do not feel sad. I feel nothing.

I recall fleetingly an only child unable to remember ever holding the hand of his father, a man who had wanted to paint and never did;

no recollection of seeing joy in the eyes of his mother, a timid soul who wrote poems and arranged dried flowers. If I misbehaved, which was rare, she would look at me with sorrow and shake her head. My father's chin would drop and they would grow motionless like refugees trapped between frontiers, the steel teeth of some disgusting despot behind and, before them, the chill picture of long avenues lined with high walls and closed doors. If you have intellectuals for parents I would advise anyone to run away. Pack your bag. Get out before they sully your mind. If they mention suicide, encourage it.

It was Marten who understood the metaphysics of the six o'clock news. He showed me how to walk on the grass. *He* was the Pied Piper, the key that enters locked doors, a missionary from another mind zone. He was seventeen and drove a yellow sports car. I was sixteen and sat at his side as the road uncurled at a white house with a window on the top floor seductively open.

He knocked. No one was home. I kept watch while Marten climbed the façade and, within minutes, was inviting me in like an eager host. Everything inside the house was white: white chairs, white sofas, white carpets, white walls. In the cupboard there were almonds, dates, figs in syrup, red wine that slips down easily and changes the mind's focus with peculiar stealth. We played music.

"Rigoletto," said Marten.

He made a joint. I smoked marijuana for the first time; it was a time of first times. The afternoon was charged with the sound of laughter and cellos; wine drops like spots of blood; broken figs, oddly biblical. The light was golden, filtering through the window shades like falling pollen. I looked at the white paintings on the white wall

173

above the white sofa: three square canvases, stains of darkness below surfaces patterned in crude brush strokes.

"Do you like them?" Marten asked.

"I suppose."

He stood close at my side, his head at an odd angle. "Are they art, or decoration?"

"Maybe they're both."

"That would depend on your...experience."

"Experience?"

"Experience makes the abstract tangible, and the tangible shows you that what it all adds up to is nothing at all."

"Art?" I asked him.

"Everything," he replied.

He laughed. And I laughed.

We abandoned the drawing room, chased each other up the white marble stairs. I followed him from room to room. He tried on jackets and hats, tossing them aside, knocking over tables and lamps. A mirror was broken. There was hair in a hairbrush in the main bedroom but no photographs. On the long flat surfaces stood unrelated objects, randomly placed: an art-deco figurine, a conch shell, a black vase with wooden flowers.

Marten was filling a briefcase with jewellery, a watch, credit cards, a gold chain. He found some banknotes, fanned them out and fanned himself before dropping the money in the bag. His fine pale hair was lit by shafts of silver light; his dark eyes subtle and mischievous as they met mine.

"What are doing?"

"What do you think I'm doing?"

"You're taking things."

"You have to live, Tomas."

"But it's stealing."

"Stealing," he said. His smile had gone. There was a moment of silence, hurried seconds possessed by hurried thoughts: I had been working on a painting at school, a large oil of a man crossing a river from a landscape forested by trees to a metropolis of flat sombre buildings. The man's face, partly hidden, was my own face, a face from the future. Red wine and dope were two motor-cycles racing around the rim of my brain. I could still hear Verdi still, faintly in the background.

He removed from his bag the gold necklace and clipped it on me.

"I don't want it," I said.

"But you must."

"Why?"

"You possess it now. It's yours."

I tried to take the necklace off but my fingers were all thumbs and I couldn't undo the clasp. I watched Marten as he examined the art-deco figurine. He used it to sweep the vase of wooden flowers from the shelf. He smashed the figure against the long mirror in the wardrobe, breaking the glass. Clothes spilled from drawers, long coats were fleeing like phantoms from open cupboards. In each chip of shattered glass my expression was different. The gold chain felt heavy around my neck.

I followed him back down stairs. He was moving faster; a film speeded up. He dragged the table and chairs to the centre of the living room, added cushions, magazines. He found a bottle of brandy and two glasses.

"I will give you a tip that you will remember for the rest of your life: Always stay for the extra drink."

He tipped a measure of brandy in each of the glasses and handed one of them to me.

"To art," he said.

I glanced about the ruins. "But why?" I asked him.

"Why?" he repeated. "The whole world wants to know why. There is no why. There just is."

He poured the rest of the brandy over the wreckage. His eyes blazed as he lit a match. I watched the match burn as if hypnotised and, as it was about to burn his fingers, he tossed it into the air. The dying match landed and became a nest of orange flames that reached for us like dancing serpents, chasing us around the room and out through the open door.

We drove back through the woods in the yellow car. The sun had gone down. The sky was black. The early stars were appearing. "If you see the moon through trees you will be struck by a spell," Marten said and I turned my head to peer back at the white house, a ball of fire vanishing behind us.

Fifteen

The tentacles of the night are wrapping their arms about me, the old city streets drawing me into their dark mystic calm. Everything seems better at night. We look better; feel better with a glass or two.

It has been a long night, the time consumed by my jeremiad. Words. How many words do we speak in a lifetime? How many of them matter? Everyone I have ever met believes they have a story to tell; living by their own lights, they trust in their uniqueness and it is this that saves them from suicide. Anton was always talking about the autobiography he was going to write, a frank and witty account of his triumphs and follies, his bid to reach the stars. The novelty and pathos of his script will be so inspiring the souls of his readers will be heartened and his own life will be enriched by the literary respect he justly deserves.

Life is a lantern theatre filled with illusion. We are fake protagonists on a stage where the props are decomposing before our eyes. The haunted street lights cower in the dark. Walls are crumbling. The sidewalks are broken. The gutters are awash with unknown amoebas. There, on the corner, stands the liquor store owned by the Armenian with unruly teeth, closed now, boarded up like a coffin waiting to be lowered into the earth. Opposite, below a brass lamp with missing panes, there was once an antique shop where Helena bought the blue vases that decorate the fire mantel in the dining room. The sound of a helicopter straining over the Palace makes the silence of the Old Quarter almost palpable.

I am retracing my footsteps, approaching a bar with barrels piled in pyramids, faded playbills from forgotten plays, a low vaulted ceiling, the brotherhood of outsiders and insomniacs. It is past 1.00 and the word *SOUP* is scribbled on a blackboard.

Inside the smell of smoke welcomes me home. A table with a cracked marble top waits in the corner as if I am a character in one of those forgotten plays and the table will always be vacant. Music plays. The muffled voices still the echoes in my head.

I was thinking about Helena's call when a fat man wearing a fez appeared, bowing from the waist before dipping into the chair opposite.

"You won't mind if I join you," he said.

He was short, grotesque in a long robe and wore a moustache shaped with the care of plucked eye-brows. Layers of flesh tumbled down his face where they had settled in the vanquished expression of the unlucky gambler. My immediate thought was that of annoyance. I imagined I did not want company. The truth was, like the presence of a despised spouse, any company was an improvement on another hour alone.

The Turk snapped his fingers and, in his own good time, Georg, the waiter, brought a bottle of wine and took my order, wiping the table with a soiled apron.

"You do not remember me. It was long ago. We are prisoners of the past," my companion said and shrugged. He had thick, mauve lips and moribund eyes rimmed in black like a stage Turk. I did not remember him although, in a way, I did.

"The past is another century," he continued. "I was loved and respected. People invited me to their homes."

178

He poured the wine, taking small, fast sips as if it were medicine, holding the glass between the fingertips of both hands, as you would hold hot tea.

"If I sold five grams they received five grams. I never cut. I never have complaints."

The soup came, steaming in an earthenware bowl: potatoes, beans, strips of something resembling meat. The bread was stale, but the hour was late. The Turk's conversation focused inward, as did my thoughts. I was happy, if such a thing is possible, just sitting there listening without listening, remembering Marten and that day long ago in the white house: my unspoken bond with Helena. It was to her that I had given the gold necklace I stole and the smell of smoke about my fingers grew more noticeable whenever she wore it.

We are products of the past, of our parents' minuscule values. Their death liberated me. My father was a bookish man with no time for books; a scholarly individual dwelling in the vacuum between opposing opinions, understanding both; tallying figures in a minor position by day; musing on the paintings he never painted; the chess moves never made; the journeys to foreign lands traced through the pages of library books. He wore jackets with patched elbows, ties marked by the fingerprints of time. His shoes had thick soles. Mother made her own dresses, rice dishes, dumpling dishes, wheat dishes, cheap dishes. We were a modest family of tedious sincerity and copious inhibitions. We did not enter the homes of our neighbours, nor did they enter ours, but we cared what they thought without knowing what they thought or, indeed, whether they thought about anything at all. We swore by the six o'clock news; returned those library books early. We maintained a firm grip on the pennies as if

179

each little coin were a precious bird we wanted to cage. "You must think of the future," my mother said and she did and the present trickled invisibly through her busy fingers. My family did not suffer poverty but the towering anxieties of the petit-bourgeoisie.

Now, I am rich. With my numbered accounts in foreign lands, I don't have to fret over piddling trifles. The Lion has been generous with his underlings. We're all fat cats now: the bureaucrats and deputies; heads of privatised utilities; house agents, bankers, advisers, lawyers; everyone importing luxury goods; the men who sit at computer terminals moving money; the companies creating statistics, opinion polls, information, free magazines; Sun Signs, How To books, What To Do books; books on how to work out who you were in your last life and what to expect in the next, assuming this one's already a fiasco. We have made fortunes telling fortunes; producing the intangible, the fruitless and the futile. Hate me, if that's your need, but believe me: money's where it's at. It's the rich widow who looks well in black. We live in an age that means nothing; which has invented nothing but subtle rearrangement; an age where the only art is marketing. What money does is show you there's no exit except death and no meaning beyond endurance. No question is ever answered. Problems are resolved, or not resolved, at the end of a trail of errors. Within the chaos money creates the façade of logic. The poet Horace said: If possible, honestly; if not, somehow, make money. Money's an umbrella in the rain; a safe harbour; a virgin; the glimpse of an illusory future. Money = autonomy. The poor talk about it incessantly and always underestimate its value.

My father did, tainting me forever. His God was security, a divinity that kept him from painting his paintings and rushed him off each day with the newspaper turned to the crossword, a clone on the morning metro, vaporising his hopes, paying his taxes, the payments on the little car that served so well when he took Mother on their last Sunday drive. She wore the dress saved for special occasions; fingernails coloured a dainty shade of pink. There's something touching seeing the dead with painted fingernails, and I couldn't help but wonder if Father had done it for her, his last and solitary opus.

Are the world's great unknown artists men like my father, those too timid to paint, write, compose? It's no coincidence that celebrated artists are renowned for their eccentricities, perversions, depravity, drunkenness, drug addiction, cross- dressing, stabbing out cigarettes on human flesh. Artists like aristocrats have the confidence to pursue their insanity, while the poor slob watching the time clock holds fast to the stale breath of other people's opinions.

The Turk understood these things. It was apparent by his crestfallen expression. He was a man who had started with nothing, amassed a fortune, then lost it again. He had been staring at me mutely for some time and now his mauve lips opened slowly, as you would open the covers of a priceless book.

"You are Monsieur le architect," he said, his voice lacking emotion.

I nodded my assent. "For my sins," I replied.

"We all have those, Monsieur."

"Indeed."

He was looking at me as a child might an accident victim. Lines creased his smooth brow and in his porcine eyes was a pained aspect that was almost endearing.

"Why did you build the Palace on the old park?" he asked, as if the question had never been asked before.

"It was my destiny," I said.

I finished my meal and called for a cigar.

The Turk waved away the waiter. "I have some. They are the best. Please."

We sat in silent ritual, biting off the ends, sucking the flame over the tips in swift intakes of breath, watching the smoke coil over the low ceiling in patterns that reminded me of the sketches I had drawn as a boy: abstract figures that mutated into trees, the trees forming surreal landscapes that covered pages and canvases, wooded hills, weeping willows in puddles of tears, apple trees laden with human heads and human hearts. My first serious painting showed a sweeping panorama of pines fading into the abyss. In Austria they celebrated the arrival of Nazi Germany by planting trees in a pattern of pale and deep-hued foliage and today, with most forests gone, a dark green swastika remains branded on the hide of Europe.

Trees epitomise destiny. Lao-tsu said every man in his life should have a son and plant a tree. I have attempted both. Trees are the key to life; they bear the shape of a key, a clue to their secret. In Spain, there are olive trees planted by the Romans. They have been destroyed many times, in fires and pestilence, but the roots run so deep they remain alive and, in their own good time, push out new shoots that flourish again. Should you take the winding track from the Ampurdan to the coast you will see these bewildered Minotaurs grazing on the dark hills above Cadaqués where Marcel Duchamp had once seen chess moves in the pull of the waves and Salvador Dali swam in a pool shaped as a giant penis picturing time as a Camembert cheese.

When I first put a wall around the common, I imagined trees carved from marble to reflect the elms on Victory Avenue. The wall was eventually constructed in blocks moulded from oil waste - regardless of the naïve posturing of the former Fire Chief - but the spirit of my idea remains in the fibreglass trees adorning the surface.

I had started with the trees and, when the last trees began to wither and die, I gazed into the mirror and what I saw was the bronzed, contented face of a man just back from holiday.

I had been in Athens on business. It was where the cough first became a nuisance. The shroud of fumes stretched over the rooftops was so vast and permanent the imaginative Athenians referred to the cloud by the name *Nefos*. It ate the features from the marble monuments. It turned the rain to acid. It killed the algae in the sea. Their cloud was like our cloud but our cloud has no name. Our cloud does not exist. It is a psychosomatic cloud we are seeing and breathing and tasting every day.

Helena joined me and we spent two weeks in the Dodecanese. We found a pension without a telephone, a room with a window that opened on to a long, natural bay and I dreamed of caging a canary and planting some basil in a pot. The sun turned amber as it dissolved into the hills, the curl of the waves lit red like a whore's lipstick. In the square, the men smoked pipes, hunched widows in parody of Madame Raimonde and Madame Sorulos walked arm in arm, boats rocked in the cradle of the motionless sea.

We ate fish and drank pitchers of yellow wine. We slept on the rocks like two clams. Helena swam and I watched as she made slow, over arm strokes, cutting through the water, leaving barely a ripple. She went a long way out into the bay and as I began to worry, she heard my thoughts and swam back again, cramping her long toes to climb gingerly over the rocks. She wrung water from her hair, then shook her head, showering me in rain drops. I rubbed cream on her shoulders and down her spine.

"Make love to me."

I kissed her neck, her ear. She rolled over and held me as someone drowning clings to flotsam. The tears on her cheeks tasted of retsina and her eyes in the sunlight were a blue I had never seen before. We made love and it was like returning home after a long journey. I wanted to fill her body with new life, another Cristian, but like the algae in the sea my seeds were dying.

"Let's stay here, Tomas," she said and the sound of my name always came as a shock to me when she used it.

"In Greece?"

"Anywhere. Let's learn Indonesian. We'll go and live in Sumatra. Somewhere empty."

"What'll we do?"

"Live."

"Live?"

"Live, Tomas."

I thought about this with the fear of the old slave facing liberty. We had money. There was nothing to stop me except some overpowering sense that there was something still for me to do and only when I had done it would I truly be free.

It had been very hot in Greece that year, and it was unusually warm when we arrived home. Autumn came as a relief, although the elms on Victory Avenue were late shedding their leaves and that winter we had snow for the last time. The wind blew in mournful gusts. The city was a reflection of the people and the people the city. We were mutually attracted and repulsed, inter-dependent like lovers who share the same bed after the love has crumbled to dust and the dust has lifted on the withering wind and has gone. The snow covered the trees, the gables, the five domes on the Palace of Democracy. The snow blew in doorways and hallways and around the flickering street lamps. Children made snowballs and snowmen and everyone said what a beautiful city it was.

That was five years ago. My life has been tormented by units of five. The pentangle has five sides. Cristian was born five years after Helena and I married and left us five years later at the age of five. By now, we could have adopted five children and they would have built five snowmen that would have shrank, melted, disappeared as the weather changed.

The days grew warmer, too warm for spring, a warmth without sun, like the heat through the plastic walls of my office. The sky was sombre and the leaves on the elms along Victory Avenue forgot to grow. They stood there like the bougainvillaea I had planted, arms outstretched in hopeless abandonment. Then, the arms fell off. The bark peeled away. The roots rotted. The trunks rotted. And the trees crashed and crumbled across the elegant boulevards.

One of the banks collapsed. Angry investors stood outside waving fists. The directors had gone. The old families who had first built houses in the hills rekindled the fire of their ancestral blood and set out like their forebears in search of fresh horizons. Apartments were trimmed in sale signs. It was gradual like ageing. It's all so obvious now, five years later, when you look back. You just don't register the changes as the changes are happening.

After the first bank collapsed, another collapsed. The manager committed suicide. There were lots of suicides. They climbed high buildings and threw themselves off. They jumped in front of underground trains and commuter trains clutching scratch cards and tabloids full of tits. Small businesses were turning closed signs to empty streets. People began to hoard food. A woman of eighty-three was hacked to death by a thief who took nothing but a box of groceries. Plants on balconies died. The ivy on old walls died. Dogs left behind ran wild in packs. The wind blew stronger, whispering messages. Flights to everywhere were booked up. It was easy to find a seat on the monorail. Anton left with Sofie and the children. The King went into exile, leaving his second wife to host the Royal Breakfast Show without him. The neon signs over restaurants and bars shivered and went out. Waiters jumped ships in far away ports.

According to government statistics, there had never been homeless people in our city except those few extroverts who exercised their human rights by residing in the elements. Now, they moved out of the elements into the unoccupied buildings in the Old Quarter where the poor were busy knocking down walls, invading the neighbouring slums to make their own slum bigger. Television and takeaway food had dulled their brains. They lacked the will to migrate

186

across town to the villas in the hills, all boarded up like crates waiting to be shipped across the sea. It's said the poverty of the labouring classes is the poverty of their imagination. Perhaps their fundamental poverty is poverty?

The Evergreen Alliance, behind in the polls for fifteen years, began to thrive, making posters and pennants, messages of hope that filled car windows, the fronts of closed down shops. They painted their cars green, the factory gates and empty banks, letter boxes, lamp-posts, fire hydrants. They dyed their clothes green and their hair and on days when the sky wasn't yellow it turned green as if in approval and glowed in the dark.

It is the role of the Opposition to automatically gainsay everything said by the party in power. As the party in power distorts truth in order to tranquillise the fears of the good citizenry, we can assume everything said by the Opposition is founded on fact. Once this is understood, we vote them into office where, no longer the Opposition, they are forced into the Government position of prevarication and deceit, this being countered by the integrity of the new Opposition.

This conventional form of *popular* democracy, however wretched, had not functioned with any degree of success at home because the Evergreens had always been weak and the Lion had never taken them seriously, a snub more effective than any insult. The Great Mason had learned from the philosophy of his heroes that it is easier to convince people with a great lie than a small one. He has been telling us for twenty years that the economy was in secure hands; there is no hole in the ozone layer, and oil tankers do not need double hulls because they do not crash into the rocks and when they crash into the rocks the oil spillage is not dangerous to sea life. Teenage factory girls in third world sweatshops *choose* to work for forty-five cents an hour. It makes no sense to the poor TV viewer in his malodorous tenement when the government sells bomber planes and nuclear technology to an ideological enemy where the ragged-arsed peasants are starving until you appreciate that the men in government and the men on the boards of the corporations are the same men, interchangeable, blood brothers in grey suits and business ties.

They tell you what you want to hear: lies or truth, it makes no difference which, as long as you stay tuned to the Royal Breakfast, eat your monosodium slow poison and save your abuse for the fat wife and drug-dulled children studying the roots of hip hop on an educational endowment. The neighbours? Fuck 'em!

They and we have lost all moral restraint; all sense of common human decency. Our world is overwhelmed by mass hunger, ethnic wars, critical levels of over population and tragic, unstoppable contamination. We have entered the third millennium of the Christian era and tuna fishermen are still slaughtering dolphins snared in drag nets because it's quicker and cheaper than setting them free. Regardless of market dips and rises, we are tottering on the brink of the worst economic and social catastrophe ever.

What can we do?

Decisions for me appear at the bottom of a bottle. I was staring at the glow at the end of my cigar. Fire is pure yet touched by an ill disciplined greed. Every little flame wants to be a bigger flame, reaching out with fiery fingers to convert everything it touches, burning its own bridges on the long march to the earth's core where the fireball god waits with his own arcane purpose. The ash from fire carbonates the soil. Flowers bloom. Trees grow again. I lit a match and stared at the flame. I had told the Turk my work was the toil of destiny and destiny is a pentangle.

He was looking at me, studying me, waiting for me to explain myself.

"I built the Palace of Democracy for the joy of sinning," I told him, and he seemed to understand.

My attention wandered around the bar. I finished the wine in my glass. Smoked. Coughed. My companion leaned forward, stroking my arm.

"I came here to work on the land," he said. "I work hard, for little money. You know, the rich make their money from slaves; slaves who work on the farms, in the factories, in the filthy kitchens of your restaurants. I work like a slave. Then, there is no work. There is no land. They tell me to go home, go back to where you come from. Go home you dirty wog. Why they say this? They are fucking bastards. This is my country. I love my country. I have a passport."

He removed it from the folds of his djellabah to show me. There was a tear in his eye and I envied his passion.

"I start a business. I give people jobs. I am honest man. When I say five grams they get five grams." He listed his wares, counting on his fingers. "Morphine, cocaine, heroin, barbiturates, Benzedrine, Lithium, Prozac, Demerol, Vicodin, Percocet, Xanax, White Dove E. I have uppers and downers, penicillin and quinine. A little opium for the discerning and literary; aphrodisiacs for the romantic; Buddha sticks from the hills of Thailand. If they want to fly I bring LSD from

California, mushrooms from Java, peyote from Mexico, Viagra for the limp and optimistic."

He sighed and his expression changed. "The Koran instructs us to make what we have bear fruit and multiply. We must exchange goods in fairness and make an equitable profit. I buy hashish from my brothers in Turkey where the labour is cheap and sell it in small quantities for amounts people can afford. In this way I prosper and abide by the Law of Allah. Does your own Bible not teach the parable of the Ten Talents?"

"Indeed," I said.

He looked pleased with himself.

"There, you see: there is one God. Only Allah in perfect!" he cried, slapping the table. "All the evil in the world is created by government, by their agents, the officers at customs." His eyes became pinpoints. "They hold cocaine through the winter and save it for summer when the people want to get high. If there is heroin on the street, they take it away so the man who needs it must go mad with waiting and pay more when it arrives. This is market forces. But is it moral?"

"All life is immoral," I said.

"I have a passport. This is my country. I love the Lion."

He refilled my glass, shifted in his seat, as if the object were alien to him. His features, like unknown vegetables, were growing more human. The moustache he wore made him appear louche and decadent, which he was, which was all the more reason not to wear it. He removed his oily fez and sat back stroking it.

"What does life mean? Why does Allah put us here? You know, I never go to the mosque. It is unsafe. There are people who hate me because I am Moslem."

"There are people who hate me because I am an architect."

He shrugged philosophically. "I tell you a story, Monsieur. You like."

He took a sip of wine.

"There was in olden times a wise Sultan who had a hundred wives. He lived happily. But then, there was a war and he had to lead his men in battle. His wives were all young, very beautiful, you understand, and in Turkey, of course, a woman who wears a ring is the property of one man and no other man would ever go near her."

He grinned, showing red teeth. "The Sultan thought about this for a long time and then talked to the kingdom's best goldsmith. This man was very clever: he designed a ring made up of four parts, four interlacing rings that stay together on the finger but, the moment it is removed, it falls apart. The Sultan went to war and came back a hero. There was a parade and a feast. Then, he went to his harem and called his one hundred young wives together. They stood in a long row, eyes downcast, each holding in their open palms their rings in pieces. Now, what do you think the Sultan did?"

He waited for my response, eyes merry with candlelight.

"He had them beheaded?"

He shook his head. "Monsieur. He beheaded the goldsmith."

The Turk laughed. We finished our cigars. He began talking once more but I had no further interest. Coils of smoke were wrapping themselves around the low arch of the ceiling. There was smoke wafting over the walls, from the cigarette hanging from the waiter's mouth. There was the smell of smoke in my hair, on my clothes, my skin. I coughed. A decision had been working its way into my mind. I knew what I had to do. I asked the Turk for another cigar, took the matches from the table and left the restaurant smoking.

The night was warm. I hurried through the winding streets of the Old Quarter, among shadows toppling like suicides from the cathedral roof. I saw no one. I crossed the sunken highway by the Victory Bridge and, avoiding the Pigeon Control, entered the Palace of Democracy.

In my office, the grill over the air vent came away in my hands. It was made of fibreglass, or polyurethane, or plastic, the same as the doors, window frames, decorations, internal walls, an ingenious network of reconstituted waste and all so hospitable to the flame. The heating throughout the complex runs on oil connected to tubes placed parallel to the air shafts, a flaw in the design that had occurred to me the moment the drawings were finished but there was a party that night and I just never got round to changing it.

I was puffing away on my cigar, cramming loose papers in the air vent, the vacuum drawing them away from me like kites from the hands of children. I started lighting them, tossing them in, the fire balls dancing along the chute and only when I heard the first explosion did it occur to me that it was time to go home. I had to return Helena's call, call the airport and buy a ticket. I pushed the grill back into place, nipped out my cigar and stuck the stub in my pocket.

I saw a security guard in the corridor. "What's happening?" he asked.

"I wouldn't like to say," I replied.

He hurried on.

I left the building by the side door and took the path across the Peace Garden. Smoke hung motionless in the sky above the palace, a brown curtain moving towards the hills, the stench of molten plastic unpleasant, but no worse than that to which we have grown accustomed. It will pass. Everything does.

The Author

Clifford Thurlow is the author of seven non-fiction books. *Sex, Surrealism, Dali and Me,* his iconoclastic new biography of Salvador Dali, was published to rave reviews in June 2000 by Razor Books. The Spanish translation appeared with RBA/La Magrana (Barcelona) in March 2001 and spent ten weeks in the best-seller lists. Thurlow is currently adapting he book as a screenplay for RoundTable Films. *All Things Considered* is his first novel.

Bastard Books
Daring New Literature

Don`t forget.....

More radical literature at:

bastardbooks.com